The Christmas Waffle

Monroe Strategic Capital Book One

Juliet McKinley

Trigger Warnings

Please Read.

I am not a dark romance writer- however- in chapter 13 there is a scene that many woman and girls in America find themselves facing. This content maybe difficult for some people to read, however it is the reality for many in our world and to ignore it would be a huge disservice to the intent behind this anthology.

With that being said- please approach Chapter 13 with caution. Content includes: mention of teenage pregnancy, rape by a parental figure, and other sensitive women's reproductive health issues including pregnancy loss.

Chapter One

Candy

"Did you sign up?"

Serina's voice hits my desk before she does, bright and chaotic and absolutely *not* supposed to be on this floor. She breezes in like rules were written for other people.

"Serina," I hiss, eyes darting to Asher's closed office door, "you cannot keep sneaking up here. Someone's going to catch you, and it's going to be me who gets written up."

She waves that away. "Relax. Accounting is a wasteland today. Everyone's pretending to work until the Christmas bonuses drop. I'm on a mission."

"For what?"

"For the waffle," she whispers dramatically.

I blink. "Why would I sign up for a waffle? Do they not have breakfast in accounting?"

She sighs like she's raising a toddler. "Not a waffle. A *waffle*. The charity raffle." She pulls up a picture on her phone: a flyer taped by the accounting coffee pot. A cartoon Santa is holding waffles like it's a crime scene. Underneath is *WIN-A-DATE: CHRISTMAS WAFFLE AUCTION!*

I stare. "You expect me to voluntarily participate in an auction where people bid actual money for a date with me?"

"Yes," she says without hesitation. "You'd get bids."

"I'd get pity." I tuck a pink curl behind my ear. "Or accidentally bought by someone's grandma who thinks I 'look like a nice girl.'"

Serina flicks my arm. "Candy Cane, you are a catch. You're smart, your eyeliner game is immaculate, and your boobs deserve their own fan club. Men would line up."

"I'll believe that when they do," I mutter.

"Also," she adds smugly, "social platforms don't like the word *raffle* anymore, so people say *waffle*. Trendy. Millennials. Algorithms. Whatever."

"You're twenty-six," I remind her. "You *are* the algorithm."

"Exactly," she says, "so trust me."

I squint at the flyer again. "Okay, but real question, why is this happening in November? Halloween is literally this weekend. Shouldn't this be... I don't know... December?"

Serina flops dramatically into the visitor chair. "Because, according to the committee, there were *so many* applicants this year that they moved the event up. More time to raise money, more families to help, more children to delight, blah blah, Christmas magic."

I narrow my eyes. "So they scheduled a Christmas waffle auction before we've even put away the skeleton decorations."

"Exactly!" she says, as if that somehow makes sense. "They said stretching the timeline gives everyone more festive spirit."

"Serina," I deadpan, "you cannot stretch Christmas. That's how corporations get sued."

She laughs. "Candy, please. They're trying to help people. Think of the children."

I point at her. "You don't even like children."

"I like them conceptually," she argues. "From a distance. Preferably when they're quiet."

I snort. "You're unbelievable."

She shrugs. "And yet you love me."

"Debatable."

She gives me a mischievous grin I don't trust at all. "Anyway, don't worry about signing up. It's handled."

I blink. "Handled how?"

She opens her mouth.

That's when the voice cuts through the room.

"Ms. Morris."

Serina freezes. I do too.

Asher Monroe stands in the doorway of his office, broad shoulders, charcoal suit, tie perfectly centered. His expression is controlled, but his eyebrow is raised in a way that says he's a breath away from sighing.

"Is there a reason you're distracting my assistant?" he asks.

Serina gives him her most innocent smile, which fools no one. "Just spreading Christmas cheer, Mr. Monroe. Charity events and goodwill to mankind."

Asher's gaze flicks to her phone, then to me, then back to her. "Accounting is three floors down, Ms. Morris."

"Right," she chirps, already backing away. "Going."

He turns to me. "Ms. Hart, my office."

I shoot Serina a murderous look as she tiptoes into the elevator and blows me a kiss.

I grab my notepad and follow him in.

His office is always colder than the rest of the building sleek, minimal, full of quiet judgment. He sits behind the massive walnut desk, typing something with the kind of precision you'd expect from a man who probably alphabetizes his silverware. I wait quietly, trying to slow my own heartbeat.

Asher Monroe is... a lot.

Late forties, maybe early fifties. Black hair just starting to gray at the temples in that unfairly attractive way men get rewarded for aging. Sharp jawline, tailored suits, the kind of presence that makes you sit up straighter even if he hasn't spoken yet.

NYC's Most Eligible Bachelor, according to the internet. Also the man who signs my paychecks. Which is infinitely less glamorous.

When he finally looks up, his eyes go straight to the paperclip still stuck in my bun.

Oh god.

I pluck it out and drop it onto my notepad. He doesn't smile, exactly, but the corner of his mouth *thinks* about it.

"Sorry," I say quickly. "I didn't hear you calling my name."

"You were staring at the wall," he says, dry as winter air.

"Reflecting," I lie, because "spiraling" isn't workplace appropriate.

He hums a doubtful noise. "The quarterly reports?"

"On... life."

"Ms. Hart..."

I straighten. "Right. Work."

His gaze lingers just a fraction longer than necessary, and my stupid heart does a stupid flutter that has no business happening in the presence of a man with a nine-figure portfolio and probably a walk-in wine cellar.

"This task is time-sensitive," he says, sliding a folder my way. "Client request. Schedule a call with the legal team for Friday, prep the financial summary, and make sure Jordan signs off before the meeting."

"I'll handle it."

He nods. That should be the end of it.

But he doesn't dismiss me.

Instead he studies me quietly, curiously, like he's trying to solve a puzzle without touching the pieces.

"Are you participating in this... waffle thing?" he asks suddenly.

I choke. "Absolutely not."

His lips twitch, unfairly gorgeous. "Good."

My eyebrows lift. "Good?"

He clears his throat, straightening his tie. "It's a distraction. And unnecessary."

Unnecessary. Right. Because who would ever bid on Candy Hart?

I swallow the sting. "Then we're in agreement."

Something flickers in his eyes. Not pity. Something... else. Something I refuse to label because labels lead to feelings and feelings lead to Pinterest boards, and I'm not going down that road.

"Very well," he says, voice returning to CEO mode. "If that's all? "

"That's all," I say, even though part of me wishes it wasn't.

As I stand, he calls my name again. Softer.

"Ms. Hart."

I pause.

His eyes meet mine, and for one heartbeat, there's nothing sleek or polished about him.

"You're... not someone people overlook."

Heat climbs up my throat. I can't tell if it's embarrassment or something dangerously close to hope.

"I... thank you," I whisper.

He nods once, like he's said more than he meant to. Like the words slipped out.

I leave before I can make it weird.

Which, given my track record, is a Christmas miracle in itself.

Chapter Two

Asher

Once I finish the email I've been working on, I turn to watch my assistant, who's lost in thought, staring off into the distance. I had been adamantly against a female assistant after the last one left her thong in my desk drawer and showed up at my mother's house, accusing me of cheating on her; a feat in itself since we were not and had never dated. Then, along came Ms. Candice Hart. Even six months later, I'm just as fascinated with her as I was when I first saw her in the lobby sitting in the corner with her second-hand clothes and bright pink hair. Watching my little assistant was quickly becoming my favorite pastime.

I flick a paperclip at her messy bun, and it hits and then falls onto the steno pad in her lap, another trait I find entirely adorable. Upon hire, she was issued a company tablet, which has been regulated to the bottom drawer of her desk because I have never seen her use it. She takes all notes by hand, and I can't even argue that it isn't efficient, as she has increased productivity for this office and Jordan and Elliott's.

"Ms. Hart, if we may." I rub a hand over my mouth to hide my smile as she perks up and flips open her notebook, pencil poised.

"Now, as we approach the holiday season, several things need to happen. Get with Helen in accounting. She has the budget, and you can plan all the holiday festivities. Typically, we have an office party on the weekend before Christmas with door prizes, catered food and drinks, the works. I'm not sure who we have used to decorate the office, but I'm sure Helen can locate that information as well." I pause and watch as Candy scribbles far more notes than I could claim.

I clear my throat, and she looks up, a pretty blush staining her cheeks. "Sorry, sir. I was making notes on decorations. I've been waiting for this for weeks. Christmas is my favorite holiday." Hearing her call me *sir* in that soft drawl is a special kind of hell I never want to leave.

"No need to apologize, Ms. Hart. Please get with Jordan and Elliott's assistants to coordinate our annual holiday retreat. Once we have a confirmed date range, we can discuss locations."

She nods and stands to leave, but the paperclip falls to the ground. Bending over, she presents me with the perfect peach of her backside encased in her simple black skirt. My cock instantly hardens, and I bite my knuckle to keep myself from moaning out loud. I clear my throat and slide closer to my desk as she turns around.

"Is there anything else I can do for you, sir?" She stands in front of my desk, looking like every wet dream I had growing up, and it is all I can do not to tell her to drop to her knees and open her mouth so I can feed her every inch. I clear my throat again and shake my head no. Clutching her notebook of ideas, she heads back to her desk.

I few moments later I hear her voice, "Oh! Mr. Reyes! Yes, he's available. Thank you, that's so very kind of you." Her laugh drifts through the door. "You are terrible. No, thank you. I'm sure. I brought something from home."

My door opens again, and Jordan Reyes, my best friend since college and my COO, strolls in.

"What the fuck was that?!" I snap, which only makes him grin.

"What was what? I asked if she wanted us to bring her anything back to eat. I don't know if you've noticed, but she never orders anything from the deli with the other assistants. Now that I think about it, the only employee I have ever seen her talk to is Serina from accounting." Jordan strolls into my office like he owns it. The bastard.

"Yes, Ms. Morris was up here this morning. What is this about a charity raffle?" Just thinking about anyone bidding on Candy but me makes my jaw ache.

Jordan's face lights up. "Oh, yes! They're everywhere right now. You sign up, people bid on a date, money goes to charity. Foster Inc. did one and pulled in a couple million."

He snaps his fingers. "Oh, and speaking of sign-ups. Pretty sure Serina already submitted Candy's name."

My jaw locks. "She... what?"

"Yep. This morning. Said Candy 'has the face of an angel and the energy of a Disney princess,' and it would boost morale." He shrugs. "You know Serina; she's chaos wearing lipstick."

Before I can respond, he barrels on. "And you remember Jack Foster? Married his assistant? Ended up being the smartest thing he ever did. Once the McIntyre merger hits, his net worth'll be triple ours."

I stare. He keeps going.

"Actually," Jordan says, dropping into the chair like he pays rent here, "the committee bumped the whole event up this year. Too many applicants. They wanted additional fundraising time to help more families before Christmas. So now the auction's in November."

I blink. "November? Halloween is still on the calendar."

"Yeah, well, they're calling it 'extended holiday spirit.' Personally, I think someone just got trigger-happy with the sign-up list."

My pen creaks in my grip. "Why wasn't I informed about this before it was approved?"

Jordan looks at me funny. "You were. We had the meeting right here in this office. You told us you couldn't be bothered and to do whatever we wanted. So we did." Jordan shrugs, and I can't even be mad at him. I barely remember the meeting. What I do remember is Candy had worn a candy cane sweater that dipped low between her breasts, and Jordan had been flirting with her, so I just wanted them out of my office and away from my assistant. Just my luck, the one time I wasn't paying attention to these idiots I call my best friends, I should have been.

"What has your panties in a twist about it anyway? It's not like you usually care one way or another about what we do for fundraising." Jordan is leaning back in the chair now, staring at the ceiling.

"Would you stop? Please." The chair thumps down onto the floor. I rub both hands over my face and sigh, leaning back in my own chair. "Look, I would prefer it if, in the future, you make sure I am paying attention to any decision like that. I'm not trying to ruin anything, but I worry about the legal ramifications."

"Asher, this fundraiser was with legal for two months, not to mention our legal piggyback off the Foster Inc. team. It has been legal'd from top to bottom and back again. Now, as your best friend, I will ask again. What has your panties in a twist about this fundraiser?" Jordan's tone had me groaning. He wasn't going to let this go. Sitting forward, I prop my elbows on my desk and look at my door.

Following my gaze, he starts to chuckle. "*Of course* that's the reason. I wouldn't mind bidding for a chance to go to dinner with little Miss Candy Cane."

A low, involuntary sound rumbles in my throat. I mask it with a cough.

Jordan's eyebrows shoot up. "Wow. You're down bad."

"I'm concerned," I correct, each word clipped. "For legal reasons."

"Sure," he laughs. "Let's go with that."

I shove away from my desk, but all Jordan does is laugh harder.

"Man, you have got it *bad*. Are you aware the fundraiser is open to more than just our company? Invites have gone out all over the city." Tsking, he stands, shoving his hands into his pockets. "If she does sign up, you may have your work cut out for you."

I watch my soon-to-be former best friend laugh as he strolls out of my office. I need to make a note to kick his ass later. But as the door closes behind him, I'm not thinking about his ass or the fundraiser.

I'm thinking about Candy– sweet, anxious Candy finding out she's been entered into an auction against her will.

I need to get ahead of this.

Before someone else gets the chance to touch what I haven't even allowed myself to want out loud.

Chapter Three

Candy

When Mr. Reyes leaves the office laughing, I take it as a good sign. Wrapping up my final tasks, I email Helen in accounting and the assistants for Jordan and Elliott to kick off the holiday planning. Grabbing my notes, I skim through them on my way to the break room for hot chocolate.

A smile spreads across my face at the sight of the counter. It's not fully decorated yet because it is late October, but a few early festive treats have appeared. There are ginger cookies shaped like little leaves, a bowl of mini candy canes someone dumped into a snowman mug, and a tray of chocolate-covered pretzels dusted with red and green sprinkles. It is the first hint of Christmas, and it is enough to make my heart do a tiny jingle.

Humming under my breath, I pop a hot chocolate pod into the coffee maker and unwrap a candy cane. I adore Christmas. I love the lights, the traditions, and the way even a corporate office starts to feel a little softer around the edges.

When "Jingle Bells" suddenly plays overhead, I snort into my mug. Someone in facilities definitely jumped the seasonal-playlist gun, because there is no universe where Asher Monroe approved holiday music in October. Halloween is still this week. We literally have plastic skeletons in the lobby.

Still, I hum along while waiting for the machine to finish brewing. The fundraiser flyer on the bulletin board catches my eye, so I wander over to take a closer look. I'm absorbed in the tiny print when someone clears his throat behind me.

"Excuse me. I didn't mean to startle you. My name is Torin Davis. I was told to speak with Candice about setting up an appointment with Mr. Monroe while I am in town. Are you Candice?"

I jump and whirl around. The man towers over me, easily six feet tall, with thick red hair and striking green eyes. His crooked smile, complete with a single dimple, makes him look like trouble wrapped in charm. The thick Australian accent does not help. I can only nod, causing him to chuckle as he gently pulls the candy cane from my mouth. For one horrifying second, I just stare at him. No man has ever reached for something in my mouth before and lived to tell about it. Mama would smack me sideways for letting a stranger touch my food, but I'm too startled to react.

"Candy cane got your tongue?"

"I'm so sorry. Yes, I'm Candice. I can help you with that." I grab my cup and candy cane before I head back to my desk.

Setting the flyer aside, I pull up Asher's calendar. "He doesn't have anything today, but there's an opening at three o'clock tomorrow."

"That can work." Torin picks up the flyer from my desk. "Are you signing up?"

I feel my cheeks flush. "No, I was just reading about it."

He tuts and glances at the flyer in his hand once more. "That's a shame. I'd be forced to attend if a beauty like you were on stage."

I blush deeper as I finish entering the meeting. "Okay, Mr. Davis, I have you down for—"

"Don't schedule that appointment, Ms. Hart." My heart races as Asher's voice cuts across the office.

"Sir?" I place a hand on my chest, trying to regain my composure.

Torin smirks, turning to face Asher. "Monroe," he chides. "You scared the lovely lady. Shame on you." I swear I hear Asher growl, but Torin continues. "You're still upset about Lila? I told you it was a misunderstanding. After thirty years, you're not still hung up on her, are you? Especially with such beauty nearby?"

Lila?

My eyebrows shoot up. That sounds like history. Complicated history. The kind I absolutely should not ask about. My gaze bounces between them like a tennis ball. "Maybe I should just…" I grab my phone and start to stand.

"Sit back down, Ms. Hart. Mr. Davis was just leaving." Asher's eyes flick from Torin to me to the flyer Torin is still holding. Something sharp flashes across his expression jealousy, maybe, or something older and angrier. Whatever it is, it hits him like a switch being thrown. "Cancel that appointment."

I sit so quickly my chair nearly wheels out from under me. Both men reach out, but I catch myself just in time.

I push my hair back and focus on my screen. A few clicks and the appointment is canceled. Folding my hands in my lap, I stare at my keyboard, hoping not to draw more attention to myself.

"Asher," Torin's voice is cajoling.

"No," Asher says, voice low and controlled in a way that scares me more than shouting would. "Torin, leave. Now. Before I have to make this a formal issue." Asher says, pulling out his phone.

Torin raises his hands in surrender. "Okay, I get the hint. Have a lovely day, Candy. Don't let this asshole work you too hard. Maybe I'll see you later?" He winks and saunters to the elevator.

Once the doors close, the tension eases, and I breathe easier. The silence stretches until Asher clears his throat. "Ms. Hart, I apologize for my behavior. Speaking to you like that was unprofessional. I hope you can forgive me."

"Oh, it's okay. It was surprising, but it's fine." I straighten the stationery on my desk, avoiding his gaze. He moves closer, and I force myself to stop fidgeting with my highlighters.

"Ms. Hart, please look at me." His near-whisper draws my eyes to him. He tucks a hand into his slacks and smiles softly. "Thank you. I'm truly sorry if I upset you. Mr. Davis is a sore subject. But that doesn't excuse my behavior."

I wave my hands in dismissal. "No, really, it's okay. I was startled at first, but it's fine."

"Well, thank you. I don't deserve your kindness. Enjoy your weekend." Tapping a knuckle on my desk, he heads into his office, closing the door softly behind him.

Taking a deep breath, I turn to my computer, shaking my head. People say working in an office is boring, but man, are they wrong.

Chapter Four

Asher

Saturday morning dawns bright and clear. I am more than ready to meet Jordan and Elliott at Stumptown Coffee Roasters for our weekly catch-up session. When the taxi drops me off, I see them waiting at our usual table. The baristas call out a greeting as I enter the coffee shop. Smiling, I chat with the other regulars, and my order is there when I make it to the register. Tapping my debit card to pay, I snag my order and flop into the empty chair. "Hey, fuckers. Since when do you idiots beat me?"

Jordan kicks the leg of my chair, and Elliott grins. I sip my drink and sigh as the sweet, delicious nectar warms my frozen soul. Winter in New York is no joke. We sit in silence for several minutes, just enjoying the morning. Eventually, we finish our food, and Elliott reaches into his bag and pulls out three containers.

"Okay, gentlemen. You know the rules. We each draw a piece of paper with an activity and a food for a location. If a paper is drawn, it must be done, no exceptions. Asher, you first."

Reaching in, I pull a slip of paper and read it out loud. "Axe throwing, Kick Axe Throwing in Brooklyn."

Jordan reaches into the second jar. "Gastropub, Lunch at Threes Brewing."

Finally, Elliott draws. "Dessert and Exploration, Ample Hills Creamery."

Jordan snaps. "I've heard of that place! They're supposed to have fantastic ice cream with really unique flavors. They have one, the Salty Malty peanut butter and pretzel." He mimics a chef's kiss, and I can't help but chuckle.

Pulling out my phone I bring up the Kick Axe website and book their first open slot. "We have axe throwing at eleven-thirty. C'mon, let's get a taxi."

We are forty-five minutes into a two-hour slot, and Jordan has just finished his turn. Taking another swig of my draft, I grab an axe and stand up, preparing to take my turn.

"So, Asher, did you tell Elliott about your little temper tantrum over the lovely Miss Candy Cane being asked about signing up for the Win-a-Date raffle?" Jordan's question causes me to whip my head around, and the axe flies wide, thudding against the far wall and clattering to the floor. He sits calmly at the table, smirking as he sips his beer.

"Why would it be a problem if Candice signs up? It's a fundraiser. The whole point is to get as many people as possible."

I know Elliott is genuinely confused. The more socially reclusive of our group, if we didn't drag him out on the weekends, he would spend all his time in front of his computer either working or gaming.

"I did not throw a temper tantrum!" Even to me, my protest sounds weak.

Jordan snorts. "Yeah. Okay. Right. You blew a gasket! I thought you were going to reach over your desk and punch me. Just admit it, man, you want her, and I can't wait for you to get her because this alpha male bullshit is getting old."

"Wait. Asher wants Candice? Wouldn't that be against company policy? He's her direct supervisor. Something like this could open us up to a lawsuit." Bless him, Elliott is always thinking practically.

"Trust me. I know this, and I do *not* want my assistant." I point the axe handle at Jordan before turning back to make my throw. The axe thuds into the wood, barely inside the outer ring. I sigh in disgust and walk down to pull it free.

"Look, you wouldn't be as touchy about the girl if you weren't into her. I heard about what happened with Torin. It's not like you to lose your cool like that. Also, I've seen the way she looks at you. I'm positive the feeling is mutual." Jordan grabs the axe from me and takes his stance.

"Asher, you could be opening us up to litigation. I really must insist you think this through." Elliott is visibly agitated, and I sigh in frustration, glaring at Jordan.

"Elliott, I'm not going to sleep with my assistant. Jordan is just trying to rile me up. Now, can we please get back to axe throwing? Our time is almost up, and I'm ready to get food."

"Let's make this more interesting. I bet you can't hit the target three times in a row." Jordan tosses his axe up, catching it repeatedly.

"That's stupid; the target is about three feet wide." I can't believe the words are coming from my best friend's mouth.

"What, are you scared? Chicken! Bok-bok-ba-kaw." He is grinning smugly at me, and right now, all I want to do is punch him right in his smirking face. He knows I can't resist a bet.

"I'm not scared. You have a deal. What are the terms?" Even as I agree, Elliott is protesting but shuts up when we both glare at him.

"If you win, I'll buy your lunch for the next month of Saturdays."

Okay, I can get behind this. That's not a bad deal.

"But if I win, you have to have lunch with Candy Cane every day this week."

I choke on my beer. "Are you shitting me right now?"

"Nope. Either accept my terms or admit defeat and forever be ridiculed as the man who couldn't hit the broad side of a barn." Jordan stares at me in a clear challenge.

I down the last of my bottle before standing up. "You're on, motherfucker."

Jordan is still bragging forty-five minutes later when we walk into Threes Brewing. I do my best to ignore him as he continues to brag about his victory; instead, I focus on the restaurant. Signs boast a wide selection of different IPAs, lagers, and beers, and the smells drifting from the kitchen immediately make my stomach growl. Jordan flirts with the hostess on the way to our table, and I can't help but shake my head. Snagging a menu, I start to read and see a farmhouse ale called Saison. I know that will be my drink of choice for this meal.

"Hey, folks! My name is Monica, and I will be helping you today. What can I get you started on? Our seasonal beer releases and pairings are on page two. Do you need a few more minutes or do you know what you would like?" She's perky and blonde, and you can tell that she loves her job.

"I'll have a bourbon bacon burger and fries with Saison to drink. Tall. Thanks." I put my menu back and look around the building while Jordan and Elliott order. "I wonder why we haven't come here before?" I muse out loud as Monica sets our drink order down before returning to the kitchen.

"The real question is, what will you and the lovely Candy Cane have for lunch on Monday?" Jordan sips his water, and I just shake my head and ignore him.

"Jordan, I don't think this is a good idea. The repercussions for the company can be severe. I really must insist you negate this bet. Please." Elliott pushes his glasses up before grabbing his glass of water.

"It's okay, Elliott. Nothing wrong with buying your assistant lunch, is there? Exactly." Jordan claps him on the back before moving so Monica can set some appetizers on the table.

"I fucking hate you. Let's just concentrate on lunch, shall we?"

Jordan chuckles at my curt tone.

Chapter Five

Candy

When I get to my desk Monday morning, Serina is holding two to-go cups. The office still smells faintly of fake fog from Friday's Halloween event.

"Serina, it's way too early for this."

"Here." She thrusts a cup into my hand and pulls out a newspaper.

"A newspaper? Didn't know they still made those." I set the cup down and log into my computer.

"Yes, yes. Just look." She waves the paper in my face. I sigh, taking it and flipping to the front page.

"Australian Billionaire Secures Landmark Deal in Trendy Manhattan District." The headline sits above a photo of Torin Davis shaking hands with the mayor.

"That's Mr. Davis. He was here last week." I'm scanning the article when the elevator dings and footsteps approach. "And he didn't exactly leave quietly." My stomach flips, remembering the tension between him and Asher on Friday. I still don't know what that was about, but I'd be fine never being in the middle of it again.

 "Ms. Morris, back again? Shouldn't you be downstairs reviewing accounting's reports for the week?"

Serina gives Asher a cheeky salute and winks at me before heading to the elevator. Asher shakes his head. "That girl has no shame."

I grin. "None at all, sir. And believe it or not, that's mild for her."

He shakes his head again and walks to his office. I head to the break room to make his daily latte. After knocking, I push open his door and set the tray on the sidebar. Placing the mug and paper on his desk, I turn to leave.

"Ms. Hart, block out noon to one on both our calendars. Order whatever you want from Tony's, plus my usual. We're having lunch in my office. That'll be all. Thank you."

He looks almost... resigned? Or nervous? Neither fit with the Asher Monroe I know. My throat tightens. I nod and head back to my desk, texting Serina.

Me: I think I'm about to get fired.

Serina: WHAT?!

Me: Asher blocked out lunch for us. He's never done that before. Why else would he want to meet with me?

Serina: If he was firing you, HR would be there. You're the best worker here. Don't worry. But if he does fire you, I'll swap all his coffee for decaf.

I smile, slipping my phone away.

Before long, Tony's delivery arrives. My hands shake as I knock on Asher's door.

"Come in."

Asher nods while on the phone, and I set up the food on the coffee table. I'm arranging containers when he walks up behind me.

"Thank you, Ms. Hart."

"Of course, sir." I sit in the lone chair while he lounges on the couch, watching me.

"Do you know who I was just on the phone with?" he asks.

I shake my head.

"The Christmas Waffle planner. She was reviewing donations and the Waffle Auction list."

I nod politely, confused. "It sounds like the event is coming together. Should we eat?"

Asher studies me then nods. "Yes. Let's."

We eat in silence for a few minutes before he clears his throat. "Tell me more about you, Ms. Hart."

"Oh. Not much to tell. Grew up in a small Connecticut town, went to college, dated the wrong guy twice, moved to New York, finished school, started working here."

"Family? Siblings?"

I freeze, meeting his curious gaze. "I had an older brother, Josiah. My favorite person in the world. We were inseparable. Mom called me his shadow."

I pause, swallowing the lump in my throat. "Every June, we'd go to the rodeo in Goshen. He competed in bull riding. He was good, maybe pro-level. But one year... it went sideways. I was fourteen. It broke my family. My parents still live near Goshen, but we haven't been to a rodeo since."

My voice cracks, and I sip my water to steady it.

Before I can process the emotion in his eyes, he rises from the couch and moves to kneel in front of me. "I'm sorry you lost your brother, Candy."

Tears blur my vision. "Thank you," I whisper. His warm hands rest gently on my legs, grounding me as I try to compose myself. "It was a million years ago; it's silly to be this upset. But then something will happen, and all I want to do is tell him about it and I can't. Then the hurt comes back." I manage a shaky laugh as I swipe at my eyes. "Not exactly a work-appropriate conversation. I'm sorry."

"Don't be sorry. I wouldn't have asked if I didn't want to know. I truly am sorry to hear about your brother." Asher sits back on the couch, picking up his food.

Lunches continue throughout the week. At first, I think it's just a quirk, a one-off, but every day, Asher blocks off the hour, and we sit across from each other. Each meal peels back another layer.

Tuesday, I learn he speaks fluent French, a skill his mother insisted on. When I test him, my own words halting yet passable, his smile lingers a beat too long.

Wednesday, we talk about childhood dreams. He had always envisioned working in finance, even as a kid. "I was the only ten-year-old who preferred reading business journals to comic books," he admits, making me laugh.

Thursday, I catch him watching me instead of eating. When I call him out on it, he simply shrugs. "I find you interesting, Ms. Hart." Heat crawls up my neck. Nobody looks at me like that. Nobody ever has.

I don't have a response to that.

By Friday, there's an easy rhythm to it. I arrive, set out the food, and we talk. It doesn't feel like work anymore but something else entirely. When I gather my things to leave, Asher leans back in his chair.

"I enjoyed this week," he says simply.

I swallow. "Me too."

"Same time next week?"

I nod. "Of course, sir."

I leave his office floating, warm, unsettled... and completely forgetting that the auction is tomorrow. A mistake that is going to hit me hard.

Chapter Six

Asher

"**S**he still hasn't admitted that she signed up for the auction," I growl as Jordan slides onto the barstool beside me. "I've had lunch with her every day this week, and every time I bring it up, she gives me polite answers."

He chuckles. "Have you tried just asking her outright?"

I glare at him, and he laughs harder. The bartender drops a coaster in front of us.

"Glenfiddich. Double. Thanks." Jordan's been drinking Glenfiddich since college when the rest of us got sloppy on Natty Ice.

"Why won't she admit it?" I should let it go. Candy can sign up for whatever she wants. The logical part of my brain knows that. But the primal part? It wants to forbid her from going home with anyone but me. She has no idea what she does to people. What she does to me. And I hate the idea of every man in New York lining up to take a shot at her.

"You've got it bad, you know," Jordan says, smirking as he sips his drink.

"I know. Trust me, I know." Even I can hear the resignation in my voice. "The auction's tomorrow. Ticket sales are the highest the company's ever seen. Donations are pouring in. This event should be the highlight of my year. Yet all I can think about is the fact that someone else is going to win a date with my assistant."

"Why can't it be both?" He signals for a refill.

"What do you mean?" I hold up my glass for a top-up.

"Why can't it be the highlight of your year for the company and for you? Win her." Jordan shrugs. "You're so hung up on her you can't think straight. But you can't ask her out because you're her boss, and Elliott might have a heart attack. So bid on her. No one can say anything; it's for charity."

My glass freezes halfway to my mouth. His words twist in my brain. "Jordan, you're a genius."

He just shrugs, taking another swig. "I know."

I throw some cash on the bar and stand. "I've got to go. See you tomorrow."

Jordan waves me off, and I stride out of the bar with purpose.

Before heading to the venue, I checked the event dashboard one last time. Everything was on track. Candy spent half the morning helping the committee set up the auction tables, though she barely looked at me when she left. Her nerves were obvious, even though she tried to hide them. I tug at my bow tie as I step into the ballroom. Candles flicker on every table. Raffle prizes line the left wall, and auction tables are on the right. A line of men in tuxes murmur near the auction sign-ups. The media frenzy outside left spots still dancing in my vision. Sighing, I head to the bar and order a neat whiskey.

"Mr. Monroe?" Her voice stops me cold.

I turn, and the whiskey I just sipped turns to dust in my mouth. Candy stands before me in a green velvet dress trimmed with white fluff that barely reaches her knees. The piped collar and her pink hair pinned up with holly leaf clips complete the look. She's a vision of a naughty elf, and I'm absolutely here for it.

"Here's your packet," she says, handing me an envelope. "I signed you up for the auction and included your raffle ticket. There's a Honma Beres 5-Star full set of golf clubs you might want to bid on. I put my ticket in for the all-expenses-paid Broadway weekend."

"Do I really strike you as someone who'd want fifty-thousand-dollar golf clubs?"

Candy chokes on her water, and I laugh. She probably thought they were just shiny.

"Fifty thousand dollars?" Her face pales when I nod. "I touched them! What if I broke them?"

"You didn't, so don't borrow trouble. Come on. Let's find our table."

Placing a hand on the small of her back, I guide her through the sea of tables. Pulling out her chair, I sit beside her as waiters buzz around, delivering starters and filling glasses. Candy sets her champagne aside, sipping her water.

"Ah, Ms. Hart! I was hoping to see you here."

I choke on my whiskey as Torin Davis sits next to Candy.

"Davis, this is a private event," I say, glaring at him.

"Private, yes," Torin says, patting his breast pocket. "But not exclusive. Anyone willing to donate twenty thousand at the door gets a seat."

Candy squeaks beside me, staring at her appetizer. I glance at her then back at Torin. "How did you convince Gilbert and Morrison to move off that Manhattan District contract? Last I heard, they'd rather die than give it up."

"That might've been their stance with you," Torin says smugly, sipping his drink. "But I found them quite willing to compromise."

I make it through dinner without stabbing Torin with my fork, though I'm unsure how. By my third scotch, Malorie waves me over from the stage. Leaning toward Candy, I whisper, "Showtime."

"Thank you all for joining us tonight," I say into the microphone, scanning the elegantly dressed crowd. "At Monroe Strategic Capital, we're thrilled to host you for our annual fundraiser. This event is more than a celebration; it's a tradition that brings us together as colleagues and as a community.

"This year, I'm proud to say ticket sales and donations have set records, all to support at-risk and disadvantaged youth across New York City. Tonight's auction and raffle represent our commitment to excellence and our shared commitment to giving back. So enjoy the evening, bid generously, and let's make a difference together."

Polite applause ripples through the room as I step off the stage. Showtime indeed. I return to my seat as the auctioneer approaches the podium. Candy is laughing at something Torin said.

"Care to share the joke?"

"Oh, Mr. Davis was telling me about his sister. Did you know he's a twin?" Candy grins, and it irks me that Davis put it there.

"No, I didn't. Fascinating. Where does this mysterious twin live?" I signal the waiter for another double.

"Portland, with her wife, three foster kids, and two dogs." Davis smirks as Candy peppers him with questions about the kids and the dogs.

The emcee steps up to the podium, and the crowd quiets.

"Ladies and gentlemen! Now for the main event: the Christmas Raffle and Auction! First up, we have a stunning set of Honma Beres 5-Star golf clubs! Let's see who wins." He swirls the tickets in the bowl and pulls one out.

"Ticket number 596247! That's 596247. Congratulations! Please head to the back of the room to meet with one of our Prize Verification Officers to claim your prize."

The prizes are announced one by one. Candy mock-glares at me when my ticket wins the all-expenses-paid Broadway weekend.

Before I know it, the auction begins. I grip my glass so tightly I have to force myself to set it down gently. I watch Candy intently, but she doesn't seem the least bit fazed by the progression of the evening. Name after name, male and female, is called, and she just chats as she eats small bites of her dessert.

Candy hasn't looked at the stage once. She's relaxed beside me, completely unaffected by what's coming. Finally, an hour later, it happens. Candy is standing at the bar with Serina when her name is called. She chokes on her drink, and Serina starts pushing her excitedly to the stage. Candy whispers furiously to her, but Serina grins and forces her onto the stage.

Candy stumbles to a stop like a deer in headlights next to the emcee, a glowing vision under the stage lights. But what gets me the most is that I can easily see fear in her eyes. She scans the crowd like she's searching for an escape route. Her eyes dart to me for half a second, pleading for a lifeline I cannot give her.

"This is our last entrant this evening, ladies and gentlemen, Ms. Candice Hart! Shall we start the bidding at two thousand dollars?"

I grip my glass, the condensation cold against my fingers, and keep my face neutral. Candy stands with her hands clasped in front of her, her cheeks already pink. She doesn't look at me.

"Paddle fourteen, two thousand dollars!"

I glance over. Torin Davis. Of course. The asshole leans back casually in his chair, his navy suit crisp, his paddle held high. He has the kind of confidence that's annoyingly hard to rattle, and his smirk only deepens when Candy glances his way.

"Paddle twenty-three, three thousand dollars!"

The next bidder is a bearded man in his forties, looking smug.

"Paddle seven, five thousand!"

A woman in a green dress raises her paddle, flashing Candy a dazzling smile. Candy shifts in place, trying to keep her composure.

The auctioneer's voice rises, urging the bids higher. "Do I hear six thousand?"

"Paddle twelve, six thousand!"

Some kid barely out of college lifts his paddle, looking far too self-assured for his age.

The bids climb steadily ten thousand, fifteen thousand, twenty thousand. My jaw tightens when Torin lifts his paddle again, his voice ringing over the murmurs. "Thirty thousand. Paddle fourteen."

He grins, and I swear it's aimed right at me. "She's worth every penny," he says, his Australian drawl dripping with charm.

Candy's eyes widen, her cheeks practically glowing. I can see the nervous shift of her hands, the way she glances at him then away.

I've had enough.

"Thirty-five thousand," I say, my voice cutting through the room like a whip.

All heads turn as I lift my paddle. Candy's gaze snaps to mine, her lips parting.

The auctioneer blinks, clearly caught off guard. "Thirty-five thousand! Do I hear forty?"

Silence. Even Torin doesn't move, though his smirk falters just slightly.

"Thirty-five thousand, going once... going twice... sold! To paddle one, Mr. Asher Monroe!"

The room erupts in applause. Candy drops her face into her hands, her shoulders shaking. Whether it's laughter, embarrassment, or something else, I don't know.

But I do know one thing: for one night, she's mine. What I don't know is how I'm supposed to let her walk away at the end of it.

Chapter Seven

Candy

Serina's nervous energy is grating on my last nerve. She's been fidgeting, adjusting my dress, and worst of all, messing with my hair like an overbearing older sister. I swat her hand away when she reaches for it a third time.

"Would you *stop*?"

"Just let me."

I swat at her again, glaring. "Serina, I swear to god—"

Before she can protest, my name booms from the stage. I choke on my drink as Serina squeals, grabs my shoulders, and shoves me forward.

"Go!" she hisses. "And smile!"

Stumbling toward the stage, my face burns under the glaring lights. Heat rushes up my neck, my palms going slick. The stage lights blur at the edges, and for a terrifying second, it feels like the room tilts beneath my feet. I glance over my shoulder, scanning for Serina when I get off this stage, she's dead, but all I can see is the front row.

"This is our final entrant for this evening, ladies and gentle-men, Ms. Candice Hart!" the emcee announces. "Shall we start the bidding at two thousand dollars?"

My heart hammers. I'm going to die on this stage. I just know it. The bidding starts, but I barely register the numbers climbing until the room goes silent at a staggering offer.

"Thirty-five thousand, going once... going twice... sold! To paddle one, Mr. Asher Monroe!"

My mouth goes dry. My boss just bought me.

I step off the stage, and Asher is waiting at the bottom of the stairs. Without thinking, I take his offered hand. His grip is firm, grounding me in a way I desperately need.

Leaning in, he murmurs, "Have I told you how amazing you look tonight?"

The woodsy scent of his cologne wraps around me, and my brain stalls. I can only shake my head.

"Well, you do," he says, his lips brushing close to my ear. "I couldn't let anyone else win a date with you."

My eyes snap to his, but his glare is fixed across the room on Torin, laughing with a group of businessmen.

"Ah. I see." Disappointment twists low in my stomach. He didn't want a date with me; he just didn't want anyone else to have one. For a fleeting moment, I thought he might actually like me. Men like Asher Monroe don't end up with their secretaries. Guys like him don't choose girls like me—not for real, not when it counts. I've fallen for that lie twice, and both times it hurt more than I care to remember.

I march back to the bar, finding Serina grinning like a Cheshire cat. "Candy, you just got bought for thirty-five grand! You should be celebrating."

"Oh, yeah. Break out the confetti," I deadpan, flagging down the bartender. "Cherry vodka sour, please."

Serina wiggles her eyebrows. "What's the plan for your hot date?"

"Not a clue." I take a long sip, trying to swallow the lump in my throat.

"You're sulking. Why are you sulking?" Serina nudges me. "This is prime rom-com material. Lean in and go with it!"

I glare at her. "Serina "

"Why did you walk away?" Asher's voice is suddenly behind me. My back stiffens.

I jiggle the ice in my glass, avoiding his gaze. "A drink after being on stage makes sense."

"It does," he agrees, watching the bartender place an amber liquid before him. He takes a sip then turns to face me. "Should we plan our date now, or would you rather meet for breakfast to discuss it?"

Serina chokes on her drink, but I ignore her.

"You want to have breakfast with me?" I can't keep the skepticism out of my tone, but Asher just chuckles.

"Breakfast. Lunch. Brunch. Dinner. I'll take anything and everything I can get."

Serina mutters, "That's hot."

I elbow her.

"Okay, breakfast it is. Where do you want to meet?" I pull out my phone to check my calendar.

"My driver will pick you up at ten a.m., and we'll go to Petite Boucherie in the West Village. The steak aux oeufs is excellent."

I type in the details before locking my phone. "Well, I look forward to it. You know, you don't have to follow through on the date. I'd understand if you'd rather forget it happened. Breakfast would be more than enough."

Asher leans in, tucking a strand of hair behind my ear. "Oh, sweet Candy. Nothing on this earth would make me give up this date. I won you fair and square."

Serina mouths, *hot*.

I ignore her.

Asher's eyes darken. "You're mine."

My breath catches so sharply it almost hurts. No one has ever said something like that to me, not like it meant something. Then Serina fake-swoons onto the bar when he walks away. "If you don't marry him, I will."

I groan. "Serina!"

She just smirks, sipping her drink.

I smooth the soft navy skirt of my nicest outfit, a simple blouse and pencil skirt combo that suddenly feels too plain, for the hundredth time. No matter how much I Googled, I couldn't get a clear answer on the dress code for this restaurant. I chose something work appropriate, by far the nicest outfit I own. It isn't the restaurant I'm worried about. It's him. I want to look like I belong anywhere he chooses to take me.

A sleek black town car pulls up, and I lean down, trying to see through the tinted glass. The driver steps out, tipping his hat.

"Ms. Hart? I'm here to take you to Mr. Monroe." He opens the door and helps me in.

The leather seats are buttery soft and warm under my legs. I can't resist running my hand over the surface. Outside the window, the buildings shift from my neighborhood's worn, slightly dilapidated ones to the trendy, polished architecture of the West Village.

I take a steadying breath. Ready or not, here I go.

Chapter Eight

Asher

I'm sitting at a table in the back when Candy walks through the front door. If you didn't know her, you'd never guess she was nervous, but I've made studying her a science over the past several months. She nibbles the corner of her mouth, her fingers twisting the strap of her purse. She looks half a second from bolting.

I hurry to the entrance, feeling a ridiculous sense of pride when she notices me and visibly relaxes. "You made it," I say, taking her hand and pressing a soft kiss to the back.

"I made it. It was easy to find with the personal driver and all." She blushes as I chuckle.

"There's that biting wit. I've missed it. Let's sit." I guide her to a chair and slide her in as the waiter fills her water glass and hands her a menu.

"As I mentioned last night, the steak aux oeufs is fantastic. You might also enjoy the pain perdu. But order whatever strikes your fancy."

I sip my espresso while Candy studies the menu, her expressions as captivating as ever. But soon I notice her biting her lip and glancing between the menu and her phone.

"Candy?" I keep my voice gentle, but she doesn't look up. I touch the back of her hand. "Candy, honey?"

Her big blue eyes finally meet mine over the menu.

"What's wrong?"

She whispers something I can't hear, so I lean closer.

"I missed that. Repeat it?"

"I can't afford anything on the menu," she murmurs, cheeks flaming pink as she stares at her phone. "This isn't the date. You shouldn't have to pay for me. I don't want to be a burden. I'll just have coffee while we talk."

Her words catch me off guard. I glance between her and the menu, confused. "Candy, what makes you think you're paying?"

Her blush deepens, but I press on, my tone steady. "I told you to order whatever you'd like because brunch is on me. You may not know much about me yet, but there's one thing you should understand: I take care of what's mine. That means picking you up, paying the bill, and ensuring you never have to worry about menu prices. Not now, not ever."

The waiter approaches, and I order all the popular brunch dishes, along with an assortment of fruit juices and mimosas. When the menus are collected, Candy stares at me in shock.

"There. Now, you can try each one and see which is your favorite for next time."

"Next time?" she asks, moving her hands out of the way as waiters buzz around the table, setting down drinks.

"That's correct. If I have my way, we'll visit here often. But that's a conversation for another time. For now, let's focus on today." I finish my coffee and reach for the grapefruit juice. "After brunch, we can take a walk and see some sights. Then, at four p.m., you have an appointment with a personal shopper at Bergdorf's, followed by hair and makeup. By dinner at Per Se, you'll be completely relaxed."

Candy doesn't respond as I lay out the plan. The waitstaff brings the first round of dishes, and she stares at them wide-eyed. I can't help but feel smug. My plan is perfect. By the end of the day, she will know precisely how much she deserves to be spoiled.

That smugness evaporates when she sets her napkin beside her plate and looks at me with fire in her eyes. "I am not a whore." Her voice is low, but the anger is unmistakable.

My jaw nearly drops. "Candy, I—"

She cuts me off, her voice trembling but resolute. "You may have bought me at an auction, but I never wanted to participate to begin with. Regardless, that doesn't give you the right to treat me like like..." She stumbles, takes a breath, and straightens her shoulders. "I'm still a person. I have worth, and I refuse to let anyone—especially someone I admire as much as you—make me feel less than that."

I swear my jaw is on the floor as my brain scrambles to process what I just heard. Candy starts to toss her napkin onto the table, but I catch her hand mid-motion, napkin and all. Her fingers are warm in mine, and I gently rub my thumb over them.

"Candice." I use her full name to ensure I have her attention. When her bright blue eyes meet mine, I continue, "That's not what I meant. I want the chance to pamper you, even if it's just for one night. Spoiling you isn't just for you; it's for me too. It's how I show my appreciation for everything you do for me. And I'll admit, it's a little selfish. I want to make sure all your needs are met."

I hold her gaze, watching the doubt fade from her eyes.

"If this is the only night I get, I want to make it unforgettable for both of us. Will you let me do that?"

She gently pulls her hand away and places the napkin back in her lap. "I'm not used to anyone wanting to take care of me," she says softly. "I can't promise anything, but I'll try."

I fork several waffles onto her plate then add strawberries and syrup. When I point to the sausage, Candy shakes her head and gestures toward the bacon instead. I pile some onto her plate before turning to fill my own.

We eat in comfortable silence until something she said earlier nags at me.

"What did you mean when you said you didn't want to sign up for the auction?" I ask.

"Serina signed me up. I didn't even know my name was on the list until the emcee called me on stage. By then, it would've been more embarrassing to make a scene than to just go through with it." She shrugs and picks up another piece of bacon. "Honestly, I thought no one would bid on me." She chuckles, forking a strawberry. "Guess I was wrong about that."

I can't help but laugh too. "Just a little bit." I pause, waiting until she looks up at me. "I have to be honest, though... I would've paid more."

Chapter Nine

Candy

Walking into Bergdorf's is always breathtaking. The seasonal decorations, sale advertisements, and endless rows of luxurious items arranged like a buffet are dazzling. As Asher's assistant, I'd purchased items from here before, but they were always delivered via courier and never for me.

The moment Asher and I step into the ground-floor lobby, salespeople whisk me away. Before I know it, I'm seated in a plush chair while a stylist works on my hair. Meanwhile, associates parade an endless stream of dresses for my approval or rejection. I can't help but laugh at the surrealness of it all.

Serina would lose her mind if she saw this *Pretty Woman* treatment. I snap a quick selfie and text it to her.

Me: At Bergdorf's getting the *Pretty Woman* treatment for my date tonight with Mr. Monroe.

Her response comes almost instantly.

Serina: Holy shit! Where are you?!

Me: I just told you. Bergdorf's. For my date.

Serina: OMG I knew signing you up for that auction was genius!

Me: I'm still mad at you for that, just so you know.

Serina: Yeah, yeah, yeah. Whatever. Have you picked a dress yet?

Me: Not yet. They're still bringing options.

Serina: I want to see you when you're done.

Me: Deal.

Serina: Where is he taking you?

Me: Per Se.

Serina: You're fucking KIDDING ME!!!!!

Me: No. I am freaking out. I have no idea how to act in a place like that! What if I spill food on myself? Snort when I laugh?

Serina: Who cares? It's not like you'll ever see any of these people again. Don't worry about what they think. They don't matter. Have the best time ever. Then tell me all about it when you're back home!

Me: You got it.

The hairstylist turns me around just as I send the final text, and I gasp. They've refreshed the pink in my hair, turning the pastel shade into a soft petal pink. My hair is pulled into an elegant updo, accented by a crystal hairpin in a floral and vine pattern, with a few loose curls cascading to my shoulders. I look so different it takes a moment to reconcile that the person in the mirror is me.

The stylist gently leads me into a dressing room, where dresses are brought in and discarded at an alarming rate. The racks around me bloom with every color of the rainbow. A flash of dark green catches my eye. Drawn to it, I walk over and run my fingers over the fabric. The sweetheart neckline makes me smile, and the length falling just below my knees feels perfect. I stand there stroking the soft cloth, lost in thought until the sudden quiet in the room pulls me back.

I look up to see the employees staring at me wide-eyed. Realizing I've been fondling the dress like a priceless artifact, I quickly drop my hand as if it's on fire. Maybe I'm not supposed to touch them?

"Would you like to try it on?" The stylist walks up to me, takes the dress from the rack, and drags me to the dressing room. I hold the robe they gave me when they took my clothes tighter and stare at the dress. It really is simply gorgeous. Taking a deep breath, I reach for it. I'm going to do this. I'm going to try it on.

I walk out of the dressing room, and the silence is so immediate I swear I can hear people breathing. The stylist and her three assistants just stand there staring, so much that I can't help but shift nervously from side to side.

"Does it look that bad?" I can't stop myself from asking. I thought it looked great, but maybe in this world, it doesn't.

"My dear, you look *stunning*. It is like the dress was made for you! Rachel Gilbert is very popular this season! Let's get you some shoes." She snaps, and her assistants rush forward with options. She looks them over before making her selection. "The Jimmy Choo Slingback in gold is the perfect pair. Excellent option, Elena." The assistant smiles before handing over the shoes.

I slip into them, and everyone claps. The stylist takes my hand and moves me into a twirl. "You, my dear, are ready."

I take one last look in the mirror before I'm led back into the lobby. "If you say so."

Chapter Ten

Asher

I'm standing in the lobby of Bergdorf's in my new tuxedo when Candy is led out to me, and my mouth goes dry. She's stunning in a knee-length forest-green dress, her pink hair styled in a way that's somehow both up and down. I may have waited a while, but from what I see, not a moment was wasted.

I hold out my hand, chuckling as she blushes. An attendant offers a mink shawl for the cold, and she freezes at the gesture. Taking it, I drape it over her shoulders. "I'd hate for you to catch a cold this evening."

After tipping the employees, we step into the waiting town car.

"Thank you for everything; the dress and the hairstylist. I know it must have cost a fortune, but I want you to know I appreciate it, despite how I reacted at brunch."

I reach out, cupping her cheek, her soft skin nearly undoing me. "I've never thought anything untoward about you, not once. One of your best qualities is that you speak your mind; you don't pull punches. If I had to change one thing about you, it wouldn't be that. So give me every thought in your head, Candy, and I'll hoard them like the miser I am when it comes to anything about you."

My hand slides along her jaw until my fingers find a curl. "From the moment I saw you, I knew I had to have you in my life, even if it was just as my assistant. I was hooked. Then, Jordan cooked up this Christmas Waffle idea, which still seems silly to me, but it gave me the chance I needed to finally take you out like I've always wanted. So I guess I owe him more than even he knows."

The car stops in front of Per Se, and I help her out. Leaning close, I whisper, "Now I get to show you off. Every man will be jealous you're on my arm, and they can stare all they want. Because at the end of the day, I'd kill anyone who tries to take you from me."

Her soft gasp is music to my ears as I guide her to the hostess stand.

"Good evening, Rachel. Is my table ready?" I barely hear her answer, too captivated by Candy beside me. When I don't say more, Rachel grabs the menus, and I motion for Candy to precede me into the restaurant.

I nod to a few familiar faces, but my attention stays on Candy. She's always been gorgeous, but she shines like a diamond tonight.

My regular table is in a semi-private alcove in the back, detached from the main dining area. For most, it's the worst table in the house—you come to Per Se to be seen—but I've always preferred peace over interruptions. Tonight, the privacy is perfect.

Rachel sets the menus down with a little more force than necessary before leaving. I pull out Candy's chair and settle into my own.

"What was that about?" I ask, shaking my head.

"You really don't know?" She giggles.

"Know what?" I glance after Rachel, confused.

"She was flirting with you, and you completely ignored her. She's upset you didn't pay her any attention."

"Why would I pay attention to her when I have you sitting here, looking like every dream I've ever had?"

She buries her face in the menu, her cheeks pink.

I open my own menu, scanning the specials as the sommelier approaches.

"Good evening, Mr. Monroe. We're delighted to have you back." Harrison bows low as he kisses Candy's hand. "Welcome to Per Se, mademoiselle. I'm Harrison, your sommelier for the evening."

"Good evening, Harrison. Lovely to see you again," I say with forced amusement. "But I will have to ask you to unhand my girl."

He chuckles, withdrawing. "Of course, Mr. Monroe. We have the bottle you ordered. Shall I pour it?"

"The 1990 Château Pétrus Merlot?"

When he nods, I smile.

"Yes, please. For starters, arrange an amuse-bouche selection. For the entrée, bring the braised lamb, duck, and beef. Add truffle mac and cheese, a wedge Caesar salad, and Parmesan-crusted green beans. For dessert, one of everything the pastry chef has to offer. Thank you, Harrison."

Reaching out, I take Candy's hand, absently tracing circles on her palm.

"That's a lot of food you ordered for just two people," she says, a teasing smile on her lips.

I shrug lightly, a smile tugging at the corners of my mouth. "I want you to try anything that catches your eye. If none of it suits you, I'll have the chef whip up something else, anything you'd like."

Her eyes widen, and she shakes her head with a laugh. "Asher, you can't just tell the chef what to cook. That's not how it works; they have a menu for a reason."

I laugh softly. "Candy, it's not about showing off or breaking the rules. It's just the reality of how my world works. The amount I spend here ensures the chef is happy to accommodate." I squeeze her hand gently. "But it's not about the money; it's about making sure you have everything you could possibly want tonight. No limits, no constraints. This evening is about you."

Course after course comes to our table. Some are enjoyed with a smile, while others are dismissed with a nose wrinkle. I catalog every expression that crosses her face for when we have to go back to a more formal relationship. I drag the dinner out for as long as I can, desperate for every minute I can get. "Why don't we go for a walk? Burn off some of this delicious dinner?"

She chews her bottom lip. "I don't know. The weatherman said it was supposed to start snowing tonight. I don't want to get caught up in it. These shoes are not exactly nature friendly. They are gorgeous and weirdly comfortable but wouldn't fare well in the snow."

"Well, it's not snowing now, and my house is just a few blocks away. If things start getting nasty, we can head there, and I will call my driver to take you home. How does that sound?"

As I stand, I offer my hand, feeling another pull to keep this night going as long as possible. "You know," I continue, my voice softer now, "sometimes you just need to take the risk. Plus, I can't imagine a better way to spend the evening than walking with you."

Candy looks at me for a long moment, eyes glimmering with something I can't read. Then she nods slowly, a smile tugging at her lips. "All right, let's go for a walk. But if I slip in the snow, I'll blame you."

I chuckle, extending my arm to her. "Deal. And I'll carry you if you do."

She rolls her eyes but places her hand in mine, standing as we move to the restaurant's exit. The cold air hits us immediately, but it's refreshing, making the warmth of the evening linger just a bit longer in my chest. The streets are quiet except for our footsteps on the pavement. The glow of streetlights reflects off the wet sidewalks, and the promise of snow seems to hang in the air, as if the world is waiting for it to begin.

We walk in comfortable silence for a while, side by side, not feeling the need for words. It's one of those moments where nothing needs to be said, and the only thing that matters is being near each other.

The distant rumble of thunder in the sky cuts through the calm night. I glance up and feel the temperature drop a few degrees.

"Looks like the snow's coming sooner than we thought," I murmur, squeezing her hand gently.

Candy shivers slightly but doesn't pull away. "Maybe just a few more blocks," she suggests, her voice playful, but I can tell she's not sure about it. I can see the storm rolling in, dark clouds creeping across the skyline.

"We don't have to continue, Candy. You're the one who has to be comfortable."

She stops in her tracks, turning to face me. "I'm fine," she says with a smile, but a twinkle in her eyes tells me she's enjoying this enjoying being out in the night with me, away from the noise of the city.

I nod toward the building at the end of the block. "Come on," I urge. "Just a little farther and we'll be inside."

We take the last few steps toward the lobby of my building, the wind picking up just as the doorman opens the door. The warmth of the lobby envelops us, and I let out a breath I didn't know I was holding.

I glance out the window the moment we step inside, watching as the first few snowflakes fall. It's soft at first, but I know it won't stay that way long.

"Shall we go up?"

Chapter Eleven

Candy

Standing in the lobby of Asher's building, I'm faced with a choice. One I never thought I would have to make. Anyone who has lived in New York for over a day can tell that the storm brewing outside will be massive. If we don't call now, there is no way a driver can get me home to my tiny apartment.

Asher's warm, steady presence beside me makes the decision even harder. I look up at him, his handsome face framed by the soft lighting of the lobby, his jaw set in quiet determination. He's waiting for me to speak, but I'm too caught in my thoughts to form words.

I know I should say no. I should be sensible. But there's something about how he's looking at me. He seems so genuinely concerned but is not forcing the issue. His warmth, the way he's always cared for me, feels like a safety net, but it's also a reminder of the line between us. I'm his assistant. I've been keeping my distance, holding on to the boundaries that should never be crossed. I'm not someone who mixes business with pleasure, especially not with someone like him.

But the storm is picking up, and the temperature is dropping fast. I glance at the snowflakes beginning to drift down, thickening the air. There's no way I will make it back home tonight, and I don't want to be stuck alone in a hotel, especially when the only option is to brave this cold without him by my side.

I look up at him again, unsure whether to feel relieved or nervous. "I guess... I guess I'll come with you."

Asher's expression softens, a smile curving his lips, as if he's relieved I'm finally willing to give in. He holds out his hand again, and I take it without hesitation, the warmth of his touch reassuring even as my nerves spike.

We walk to the elevator in silence, my mind racing as I try to calm my thoughts. What does this mean for us? Is it just the snowstorm, or is it something more? I've always been careful to keep things professional between us, but now... it's starting to feel like the lines are blurring.

The elevator doors close behind us, and I can feel the space between us shrink even more. The ride is silent, the space between us charged with unspoken thoughts. My mind races. This is risky. What if I mess everything up?

"You okay?" he asks quietly.

I nod, then hesitate. "I can't lose this job," I admit softly. "I really need it."

"I understand," he replies, his tone reassuring. "This won't affect your job. I promise."

His words offer some comfort, but my nerves remain on edge.

I want to argue, but his calm assurance melts the tension in my shoulders. I'm so used to being the one in control who keeps things professional and distant. But with him... it's different. There's a magnetic pull I can't deny.

The elevator dings, and we step out into the hallway. My heart beats faster as Asher leads me down the corridor toward his penthouse. The door clicks open softly, and he gestures for me to enter first.

I'm struck by the quiet luxury of the space; everything is sleek, modern, and perfectly put together. It feels... intimidating. Like I don't belong here.

I stand just inside the door, unsure of what to do next, and Asher moves past me, setting his coat on the back of a chair before turning to face me.

"Are you cold?" he asks gently.

"A little," I reply.

"I'll get you something to drink," he says, moving to the kitchen with graceful ease.

I stand frozen, the weight of the moment pressing down on me. I need this job. I can't afford to misstep.

He returns with a glass of wine, his expression soft but serious. "You're safe here, Candy. Stay as long as you need. Your job is secure."

I take the glass, the warmth of the crystal grounding me. "I don't want things to get complicated," I whisper.

"We'll figure it out," he assures me, standing close and steady. "One step at a time."

I raise my glass to my lips, the wine smooth and comforting. For tonight, that's all I can hold onto.

I stand here, feeling the quiet weight of the moment. I hear the soft patter of the snow against the windows, but inside, everything feels still. Almost like this night was inevitable, and now that it's here, there's nothing I can do to stop it.

"Asher..." My voice is barely above a whisper, but he hears it, turning toward me, waiting for me to continue.

When I don't, he steps closer, his presence filling the space between us. "We'll figure it out. One step at a time. But for now, let's just enjoy being here. Together. No pressure."

I swallow hard, trying to make sense of it all. He's right. I don't need to overthink everything. I don't need to have all the answers right now.

I raise my glass, taking a slow sip of the wine. It's smooth, warm, and comforting. Just like him.

For tonight, that's enough.

Chapter Twelve

Asher

I watch Candy roam around my space, her lithe figure silhouetted against the New York skyline. I am once again taken aback by her beauty. Every graceful movement locks me in further. She's hesitant and cautious; I only want to erase that tension from her shoulders. My pulse quickens as I step closer, the air between us thick with anticipation.

"Candy," I murmur, my voice low, capturing her attention.

She turns, her eyes wide and searching, and at that moment, I know I can't hold back any longer, but this can't be just my decision.

"Tell me no, and we walk away as if this never happened. I'm just your boss, and you're my assistant."

Her lips part in a shaky breath. "I should say no... This could ruin everything." Her voice trembles, betraying her uncertainty.

I nod, my hands curling into fists at my sides. "I know. I've told myself a hundred times this is a line we shouldn't cross."

She takes a step forward then stops, her eyes conflicted. "I need this job, Asher. I can't risk losing it."

My throat tightens. "And I can't risk losing you, Candice. Even if it's selfish."

We stand in silence, each battling our own logic, but the magnetic pull between us refuses to let go. She whispers, almost to herself, "This is reckless."

I take another step, so close I can feel her breath. "Then tell me to stop."

Her eyes meet mine, full of unspoken desires and fears. She doesn't speak.

Neither do I.

Logic dissolves, and the space between us disappears entirely. Her lips tremble beneath mine as I brush the softest kiss against them. Snagging her lips in a deeper kiss, I part them, delving my tongue into her mouth, tasting her sweetness mixed with hesitation. Her hands grip the front of my shirt, not pushing me away but grounding herself as our kiss intensifies.

I pull her closer, my hands sliding along her back, memorizing every curve. She responds, her tongue meeting mine in a sensual dance that sends shivers down my spine. We break apart for a breathless moment, foreheads touching, hearts pounding.

"I shouldn't want this," she whispers, but her lips seek mine again.

"I know," I murmur between kisses, unable to stop. "But I can't help it."

Her fingers trail up to my neck, tugging me back in. I lose myself in her, all rational thought slipping away. Swinging her into my arms, I kick the door to my bedroom open and deposit her into the middle of my bed. Her dark green dress blends into my black sheets, but her pink hair shines like a beacon against the material. She gazes at me, breathless and wide-eyed, as if torn between restraint and desire.

I hover over her, brushing a strand of pink hair from her face. "We can still stop," I whisper, my voice strained with the effort of holding back.

Her response is a soft pull on my shirt, bringing me down to her lips. "Don't stop," she breathes.

Any remaining hesitation vanishes as I claim her mouth, my hands sliding down her sides, feeling the heat radiate from her. She arches into me, and I'm lost in the sensation of her softness against me. The world outside ceases to exist as we give in to the magnetic pull between us, our need too strong to deny any longer.

I step back and help her to her feet by the bed. My hands roam, smoothing and caressing, until I find the dress's zipper under her arm, the cool metal sliding smoothly with a soft rustle of fabric. As the zipper gives way, the dress falls effortlessly, pooling around her feet. Beneath the layers of fine material, a silk and lace bustier corset is revealed, its delicate fabric shimmering in the soft light. The corset is intricately designed, the lace tracing elegant patterns along her ribs, and the silk hugs her body, its smooth texture cool. A matching tiny thong is the only other fabric to grace her body, and my mouth instantly becomes a desert.

"You are breathtaking." I pull her close to me and claim her mouth again. I hesitate for a second, thinking I'm coming on too strong, but her arms wind around my neck, tugging me closer. I rip open my shirt, and the buttons fly around the room, hitting the floor. I manage to get my belt undone without relinquishing her mouth.

I pick her up, and she immediately wraps her legs around my waist, pressing her soaked core tight against my cock. Groaning, I lie us down on the bed, pushing her thighs open and grinding against her. Lying flat, the corset presses her breasts up like ripe apples, and without thinking, I lean down to take a bite, nipping and teasing until a peaked nipple falls out and into my mouth. Laving it with my tongue, I tease and scrape with my teeth, causing a symphony of whimpers and moans in the night.

"Oh, sweet fucking hell, you are a vision. *Goddamn.*" A shudder racks my body, and it's all I can do not to rip her remaining clothes off and slam myself balls-deep in her warmth. Giving into temptation, I twine my fingers into the strings of her thong and twist, ripping it away from her body and tossing it to my bedroom floor. Leaning back, I spread her before me and look at her, licking my lips. I dive forward and drive my tongue through her folds. Candy squeals, arching up off the bed, her fingers twisting in my hair, holding me in place as I devour her as if I am destined for death in the morning and she is my final meal.

I slide a finger into her opening, curling it slightly to rub over that one spot as I lash her clit with my tongue. Candy comes, sobbing my name, and I can't help but grin against her skin.

"That's one. I'm not done with you yet, sweet pea." I slide up until we are face to face again. " I'm going to ruin you for anyone else, Candice. By the time I am done with you, you will be mine." I reach down and line my shaft up against her opening and press in, stretching her warmth as I inch my way inside. Snagging her wrists, I hold them above her head as I use my full weight to pin her to the bed. Leaning down to whisper all the things I want to do to her in her ear, I start to slowly stroke in and out of her heat until she is struggling against my hold, begging me to move faster and harder.

Hitching her leg up against my waist, I open her up farther for me. "Anything for you." I speed up, my cock slamming in and out of her soaking pussy. "I am going to come so hard nine inches deep in this pussy, and it's going to be your fault. You feel that good."

Her walls grip me as she screams my name; I can only praise her.

"That's it. That's two. Come for me again. Let me feel that pussy choke my cock. Such a good girl, coming for me. Give me another. Give it to me now."

Our fingers twine together, lips brushing, our breath mingling as I find myself getting completely lost in everything that is Ms. Candice Hart.

Chapter Thirteen

Candy

***Please note there are situations in this chapter that some readers may find difficult. Please refer to the trigger warnings at the front of the book for more information.**

"Give me another. Give it to me now." Asher's voice is rough in my ear, and I can't suppress the shiver that works down my spine. I've never come so much in my life. It's almost like he knows my body better than I do. I can't stop myself from moaning his name as he owns me.

"Please." I don't know what I'm begging for now; I just know I need something. I need more. I need Asher.

His rhythm falters, his breath coming in short, ragged bursts against my neck. I feel the tension coil in his muscles, the way he grips me tighter, pulling me impossibly closer. My body responds instinctively, legs wrapping around his waist, holding him to me as the heat between us builds to something blinding.

"Asher," I gasp, my fingers digging into his back, nails pressing into his skin.

He groans, his voice rough and desperate. Then we tumble together, bodies tightening, breaking apart, and finally shattering. The world fades; nothing exists beyond this moment, this man, and how he's unraveling with me.

The last thing that crosses my mind before falling asleep:

I'm playing with fire.

Asher Monroe is dangerous, not in the reckless, bad-boy way, but in the way that makes a woman forget herself. He's confident, relentless, and utterly wrong for me.

Deep down, I know better. This won't end in a simple flirtation. Not with him. Not with us.

And yet, as exhaustion pulls me under, I can't help but wonder... what if I let myself burn?

For weeks now, Asher and I have been reckless. His desk. My desk. Conference room. Even the executive lounge. If it had a door and locked, we tested its limits. It was a miracle no one had walked in on us, or maybe Asher didn't care. The man had a way of making me forget where we were with just a look.

I bit my lip, trying to focus on the vendor report before me, but my mind kept drifting back to this morning. Asher's hands, warm and demanding on my hips. His lips at my throat. That deep, gravelly whisper against my skin

"Ugh. I need sugar."

Serina's voice jolted me back to reality. She slumped against the edge of my desk, looking entirely over life.

"It's one of those days," she groaned. "Cramps from hell. I need something sweet, or I might actually commit a crime. You in?"

My stomach flipped.

It's one of those days.

My fingers stilled on my keyboard as I mentally counted back. The last time I—wait. That couldn't be right.

My heart picked up speed.

"Candy?" Serina frowned. "You okay? You just went, like, ghost white."

"Oh. Yeah." I forced a smile. "Just thinking."

Thinking hard.

The exhaustion, the mood swings, the random nausea I'd blamed on too many late nights with Asher, it all came crashing together.

I was late.

Oh hell.

"Actually, you go ahead," I said, waving Serina off as casually as possible. "I've got a couple of things to finish up."

She gave me a long, suspicious look, but thankfully, her need for sugar won out. "Fine. But if I don't return, assume I drowned in a sea of M&M's."

As soon as she was gone, I grabbed my phone and started a search for local family planning clinics. A few options popped up, but one caught my eye: **Willow Creek Women's Health.**

I tapped on the number, my thumb hovering over the call button.

Was I ready for this?

My pulse pounded in my ears. Ready or not, I needed to know.

The waiting room of Willow Creek Women's Health is quiet in a way that feels too loud. The soft hum of the air conditioning, the occasional shuffle of paper, the distant murmur of voices behind closed doors, none of it drowns out the thoughts racing through my head.

I grip the clipboard in my lap, eyes skimming over the intake form. **Last menstrual period. Birth control use. Symptoms. Pregnancy test needed?** The words blur. My fingers tighten around the pen. I haven't checked the box yet. **Yes** or **No**.

Across from me, a girl—barely a teenager—sits curled into herself, fingers worrying at the hem of her hoodie. She looks too small for the chair and too young for the weight in her eyes. A woman, a little older than me, sits beside her, holding her hand and whispering something I can't hear.

The girl clears her throat, and barely above a whisper, she asks, "How long do you think it'll take?"

The woman squeezes her hand. "I don't know, baby."

Baby. My stomach knots. The girl's voice is small, but something in it makes my chest ache.

She catches me looking and offers a quick, shy smile. I return it, but I don't know if she sees it before she drops her gaze back to the floor.

A chair scrapes softly, and I glance sideways as another woman sits nearby. Mid-thirties, maybe, but young. Tired. She rubs her hands together before pressing them between her knees, like she's holding herself together.

She lets out a slow breath. "Third clinic I've tried," she mutters to no one.

I blink, unsure if she's speaking to me or thinking aloud. When she glances my way, I meet her eyes.

"Doctors won't do it," she says, her tone bitter, like she already knows I won't understand. "I've asked three times. Three different hospitals. But I don't have kids, so it's a no."

I frown, confused. "Do what?"

She exhales sharply, shaking her head. "Get my tubes tied." Her voice drops, softer now. "Last pregnancy almost killed me. Doctors told me if I got pregnant again, I probably wouldn't make it." A hollow laugh. "But apparently, that's not reason enough."

Something in my chest cracks.

I don't know what to say. I'm here because I don't know if I'm pregnant. She's here because she can't afford to be.

The younger girl shifts in her chair, gaze still locked on the floor. "I had to come here," she says quietly, like it's a confession. "Because I can't get help in Texas."

Silence settles heavily between us.

I don't ask why. I don't need to.

Her fingers tighten on the hem of her hoodie, twisting the fabric as she speaks. "My stepdad." The words catch. She swallows, clears her throat, and tries again. "He said I was his. That my mom didn't care, so I should just—" She stops, inhaling sharply, like the words are knives in her throat.

The woman beside her—her sister, maybe—runs a soothing hand over her back. "She went to the police," she says firmly. "We did everything right. But by the time anyone listened, we were out of time."

I swallow hard.

The third woman, the one fighting to get her tubes tied, shakes her head. "And yet he's probably still free."

The girl doesn't answer. But she doesn't need to.

I feel sick.

The air is thick with something unspoken, a shared understanding between us. It is the quiet kind of grief that simmers beneath the surface, the kind that lingers long after the moment has passed.

A fourth woman, maybe in her early twenties, shifts in her seat near the door. She's been silent this whole time, scrolling on her phone, but now she looks up. "The system's bullshit," she mutters, like she's speaking from experience.

I glance at her, unsure if she's responding to the girl's story or the woman beside me.

She lets out a slow breath, tossing her phone onto her lap. "I'm just here for a blood test," she admits, stretching her legs like she's been sitting too long. "Already took two at home, but I need to be sure." A pause. Then, softer, "Last time, I lost it. I don't want to go through that again."

The rawness in her voice is different from the others, less bitter, more fragile. She pulls her sweater tighter around her body like she's bracing for impact.

No one speaks right away.

We are all here for different reasons. We don't know each other's names. We may never see each other again. But at this moment, in this tiny waiting room with outdated chairs and magazines no one reads, we share something unspoken.

My fingers press into my stomach, an unconscious movement, a silent question I don't have an answer to yet. I thought I was overwhelmed when I walked in here, drowning in uncertainty. But now, sitting in this waiting room, listening to these women's stories, my fear feels small.

Not unimportant. But different.

The nurse calls my name, and my stomach clenches.

I stand slowly, my legs unsteady. As I move past the young girl, our eyes meet again for a second.

I want to say something, but what do you say to someone who has no choice?

She gives me a slight nod, almost imperceptible. I nod back.

And then I step through the door into whatever comes next.

I leave the clinic, the door closing softly, but everything feels too loud. The world outside is too bright, too crisp. The paper in my hand shakes and crumples from how I've been clutching it since leaving the exam room. I stare at the small, official-looking printout, and it hits me: **positive.**

The word stares back at me, blunt, final, like an accusation. I hadn't been prepared for a truth I don't know how to face. My hands are clammy, trembling just enough to notice, but I can't stop looking at the result.

Positive.

The words echo in my head.

I see a bench near the clinic and take a seat. I don't know how long I sit there, but it feels like forever. The world moves around me, people walk by, and the sounds of passing cars fade in the background. It's as if I'm watching everything from far away, like I'm not really here.

"Didn't expect to see you here."

The voice jerks me from my daze, and I look up to see Torin Davis standing there, his usual easy grin on his face. When his eyes meet mine, it falters just a little, like he can tell something's off. He steps closer and, without a word, sits down on the bench next to me, his presence solid and warm.

Torin doesn't ask right away. He just sits there, his silence understanding, giving me some much-needed space. But I can't avoid it for much longer.

"You okay?" he finally asks, his voice a little softer than usual.

I glance at him, forcing a smile, but it doesn't feel right. "I, yeah. I just..." The words are stuck in my throat. *I'm pregnant.*

Torin's eyes flick to the paper in my hand, then back to my face. He says nothing, but I know he's putting things together. The clinic. The way I'm sitting here, not moving, not speaking.

He leans forward, his brow furrowed in concern. "What happened? The results..."

I inhale, still holding the paper too tightly. "Positive," I say, the word falling from my lips in a breathless whisper. It's almost like I don't believe it, like I'm waiting for someone to tell me I misunderstood.

Torin's reaction is immediate but not what I expected. Instead of shock or pity, he seems to take in a breath, letting my words settle into place. He doesn't push, doesn't flinch.

"Candy..." His voice gentle but firm. "How do you feel about it?"

I blink at him, my heart thudding. How do I feel? That's the question, isn't it? I look at the paper again, and everything shifts in my chest. I don't know what I feel.

"I... I'm not sure," I admit, my voice cracking slightly. "I thought... I thought I'd be ready if this ever happened. But now..."

I trail off, unsure of what I'm even saying anymore.

Torin watches me, not interrupting, just allowing me to work through it. His presence is grounding and steady.

"Whatever you're feeling, it's okay," he says quietly, and something in his tone makes my heart stutter. "You don't have to figure it all out right now."

I swallow hard, my eyes stinging for reasons I'm not ready to admit.

I haven't really thought about what comes next. I don't know if I'm ready, and I don't know if I want this.

"Thank you," I whisper, my voice barely a breath. It feels weak, but it's all I can manage.

He gives me a small, reassuring smile. "You don't have to thank me. You don't have to go through this alone, okay?"

Torin leans back, letting me sit with my thoughts. He doesn't try to fix it or tell me what to do. He allows me to breathe, think, and figure out what happens next.

And in that moment, even with everything swirling in my mind, I realize one thing:

I'm not as alone as I thought.

Chapter Fourteen

Asher

I'm running late for a meeting, something about a potential tech investment that's been dragging on for weeks, but I can't focus. Candy is all I can think about. Even Jordan has started teasing me about it.

I walk briskly down Main Street, phone in hand, trying to ensure everything is still on track when I see them.

Candy. And Torin.

They're sitting on a bench under a tree, not laughing or joking, just talking. But it's the way their bodies are angled facing each other, the quiet intimacy in their conversation, that makes my stomach drop. She's leaning in slightly, and his posture is wide open as if he's listening intently to whatever she says.

She told me she was taking the day off because she was sick, not go on a date with another man.

My steps slow as the frustration builds, tightening around my chest. I keep walking toward them, trying to stay calm, but seeing them together so close and familiar pushes me to a breaking point.

I stop just a few feet away from the bench.

"What the hell is this?" The words burst from me before I can think, harsh and unfiltered.

Candy's head jerks up, her expression startled for a split second before she smooths it with practiced neutrality. Torin doesn't move, but I can see the tension in his shoulders and the slight tensing of his jaw.

"I—" Candy starts, but I don't let her finish.

"You said you were sick, Candy. This doesn't look like sick to me. What the hell is going on?" My voice rises, raw with frustration. Anger bubbles up from somewhere deep inside, and I can't stop it.

Torin meets my eyes, his gaze hard and unyielding. "I think you need to watch your tone, Monroe,"

I turn on him instantly, my fist clenching at my side. "I think you need to shut up and leave my assistant alone, Davis."

Candy stands up quickly, cutting off any further exchange between us. She's looking at me now, her face flushed, posture tense with something I can't quite place. "Asher, I didn't lie to you; I wasn't feeling well. This isn't what you think it is. Torin was just—"

My jaw tightens. "Torin?! It's Torin now, is it? You told me you were sick, and now I find you out here with him. What's going on?" The words spill out, sharper than I intended. Anger and hurt swirl together, but deeper still, there's a painful truth I'm too scared to face.

"I'm not obligated to explain every detail of my life to you, especially not when I'm sick." Exhaustion coats her words.

Torin also rises to his feet, his body language protective. The tension between us is thick, the space electric. It's not a confrontation, but it's not peaceful either.

"Maybe that's the issue, huh?" The words slip out before I can stop them, bitter and accusing. "We've had a few good weeks, and now you're looking for your next mark. I should have known."

The moment the words leave my mouth, I wish I could take them back. But it's too late. The damage is done.

Candy flinches, her posture stiffening. Her eyes widen briefly before she closes them, and she takes a sharp breath like she's trying to hold herself together. The air feels charged, like everything we've wanted to build hangs in the balance.

"Excuse me?" she snaps. The anger in it cuts through me like a knife.

I should have known better than to let my emotions get the best of me. But the words are out, poisoning the space between us.

"You heard me." I can't help the accusations that fly from my mouth even knowing that she is not the one deserving of my ire. It's too similar, too familiar for anything close to rational to stop me. "You've always got one eye on the exit, right? Always thinking about what's next. I should have known better than to expect anything real from you."

Candy's eyes darken with something I can't entirely place hurt, fury, maybe even disappointment. "You have no idea what you're talking about," she spits, stepping closer, her face flushed with a mixture of rage and something more profound, more painful.

Torin shifts forward slightly, his chest puffing out in a way that's not just protective but almost threatening. "Asher," he growls, his voice hard, "you don't get to talk to her like that."

I barely register him stepping closer, my focus on Candy, the weight of what I've just said pressing down on me. Her lips tremble, but her eyes filled with anger and something I can't name make me feel like I've crossed a line I can never return from.

"You think I'm just some damn game, Asher?" Her words cut deep. "That I'm here to be your plaything, and the minute I'm not catering to your every demand, you throw me away?"

"No," I start to protest, but she cuts me off, shaking her head, her gaze never leaving mine.

"You've never really seen me, have you? I really was just a conquest for you." Her voice cracks, that vulnerability breaking through all the anger. But before I can say anything, she turns away, her back straight and determined, and starts walking toward the street. Her pace quickens with each step, and it feels each step she takes deepens the crater building in my chest.

"Candy!" I call after her, but my voice is swallowed by the distance.

Torin steps into my line of sight, his eyes filled with fury. He's close now, his chest rising and falling in slow, deliberate breaths. The air is tense, and I can feel the storm between us brewing.

"Listen," he says, his voice a low growl, "I don't know what you think you're doing, but that was uncalled for. You're messing this up, Asher. And for what? Because you're too scared to let anyone in? Because you're too selfish to see what is right in front of your face? If you don't fix this, she will disappear, and you'll have no one to blame but yourself."

His words hit me like a punch to the gut, and for the first time, I realize just how far I've pushed Candy away.

Before I can respond, Torin steps back and follows her, leaving me standing alone, my meeting forgotten, and I can't help but wonder.

How could she do this? How could she run straight to *him* of all people?

Torin Davis. The man who slept with my girlfriend in college and acted like it was nothing. The man I swore I'd never trust again. And now, Candy is with him? The betrayal burns in my chest, hot and unrelenting.

Was I wrong about her all along? Did I misjudge everything between us?

Torin's words echo in my head, mocking me. *You're messing this up, Asher.*

No. *She* is the one making a mistake. And I refuse to stand by and watch it happen.

But then another thought creeps in, unwelcome and sharp *What if I pushed her right into his arms?*

What if I've already lost her?

And what the hell am I going to do about it?

Chapter Fifteen

Candy

I don't make it far before the tears start. Hot, humiliating tears that blur my vision and tighten my throat until I can barely breathe.

Torin catches up to me just as I step onto the sidewalk, his hand gentle on my arm. "Candy? Hey, look at me. Look at me. Are you okay?"

I shake my head, unable to speak past the lump in my throat. My chest aches, and the weight of Asher's accusations presses down on me like a lead blanket. I wipe at my eyes furiously, but it's useless; the tears keep coming.

Torin doesn't hesitate. He steers me toward a quieter street, away from the prying eyes of curious onlookers. "Come on, let's get some air and then a taxi."

We walk in silence for a few minutes until he guides me to a bench in a nearby park. I sink onto it, my hands trembling as I grip the hem of my dress.

"I don't understand," I whisper finally. "Asher looked at me like I was nothing, like I betrayed him. I just discovered that my world as I know it has changed forever, and now I don't even have him. He hates me."

Torin exhales slowly. "Asher doesn't hate you."

I let out a bitter laugh. "You were there, Torin. You saw his face. He was furious. He thinks I lied, that I was sneaking around behind his back. And now, he—"

My voice cracks, and I press a hand over my mouth to stifle a sob. His hand settles on my shoulder, steady and warm.

"He's an idiot," Torin says simply. "A stubborn, brooding idiot, who lets his own issues blind him. And he's probably seeing ghosts that aren't even there."

I sniffle, looking at him through watery eyes. "What does that mean?"

He leans back against the bench, rubbing a hand over his jaw. "It means Asher has demons. And I'm one of them."

I frown, confused, but he just gives me a wry smile. "Back in college, I made a mistake. A big one. And Asher never forgave me for it. So seeing us together, he probably assumed the worst. Doesn't mean he's right."

My stomach drops. "You think Asher thinks... that you and I—"

Torin shrugs. "Wouldn't be the first time he jumped to conclusions. But Candy, you can't let him push you away over something that isn't real. You have to talk to him. Set him straight. Because if you don't—if you let his anger win—then he's going to lose something he really doesn't want to lose."

I want to believe that. I do. But the memory of Asher's cold, hard stare is burned into my mind. "And what if he doesn't listen? What if he's already made up his mind?"

Torin sighs, watching me for a long moment. "Then make him listen."

I stare at my hands and the now mangled sheet of paper in them, my heart a tangled mess of hope and hurt. I don't know if I have the strength to face Asher again to fight for something when I don't even know what my future is gonna look like.

But the thought of walking away? The idea of letting him believe something that isn't true?

That hurts even more.

I badge into work the following day, my eyes still red and puffy. Swiping at my nose, I scan my card for the elevator. My stomach churns as I step inside, dreading the confrontation I know is coming.

When I arrive, Asher is already in his office, standing behind his desk, his jaw tight, his eyes dark with something unreadable. The tension in the room is suffocating as I close the door behind me. I don't move away from it, keeping the distance between us.

"We need to talk," I say, my voice softer than I intend but steady.

Walking around his desk, Asher leans back against the front, arms crossed. "Oh? About what? About how you lied to me about being unwell? About how you ran straight to Torin?" His voice is sharp, dripping with contempt. "Or about what a fool I've been for thinking you were different?"

I flinch at his words but push forward. "Nothing happened with Torin, Asher. He was just trying to be a friend, and I didn't run to anyone; I was truly unwell."

His laughter is cold, humorless. "A friend? That man doesn't know the meaning of the word. Do you think I'm stupid? That I don't know exactly what kind of man he is?" He steps closer, his presence overwhelming, crowding me against the door. "Tell me, Candy, did he comfort you? Hold you while you cried? Did you let him kiss you?"

"Stop it!" My voice cracks, and I shove at his chest. "You don't know what you're talking about. I was upset, and he was there. That's it."

He shakes his head, running a hand through his hair. "I don't believe you."

Tears prick my eyes, but I refuse to let them fall. "I came here to tell you the truth. To tell you that—" My throat tightens. This wasn't how I wanted to do this.

"That what?" he challenges. "That you regret getting caught?"

My breath hitches. "That I'm pregnant."

The room goes still. His face pales for a split second before hardening. "Don't. Don't stand there and lie to me."

I let out a shaky breath. "I'm not lying. I found out yesterday. I was going to tell you, but then—"

"Were you going to tell me before or after your date with Torin?" His eyes blaze with something dark and dangerous. "You've obviously been playing me for a fool for weeks now. You expect me to believe this baby is mine? You've been flirting with Torin since the first day in my office. He obviously felt the same since he was willing to pay so much for you at the auction. How long has it been going on? Weeks? A month? Did he bribe you to try to get onto my schedule? Did you two laugh at me in bed at night?" His voice grows louder until he is practically shouting at me.

Pain lances through me at his words. "You're the only one I've been with, Asher. How can you even ask me that?"

He stares at me, his breathing ragged. "Because I don't know what to believe anymore."

Something in me snaps. I shove at his chest. "Then let me make it easy for you. Believe whatever the hell you want."

He grabs my wrists, yanking me against him. "You drive me insane, Candy."

I glare up at him, my pulse hammering. "Good. Now you know how I feel."

Chapter Sixteen

Asher

Candy glares up at me, her cheeks flushed pink to match her hair, and she looks more beautiful now than I have ever seen her. Her chest rises and falls in quick, uneven breaths, and I slam my lips down on hers.

She shoves against my shoulders before melting against me, her arms moving around my neck. Sliding my hands down her sides, I cup two handfuls of her sinful ass before lifting her against me. Her skirt rides up as she locks her legs around my waist.

Turning, I carry her until I get to my desk; one sweep of my arm, and all the paperwork ends up on the floor. I drop Candy onto the desk, my body pressing between her thighs as I devour her mouth. She gasps against my lips, her nails scraping down my scalp as I grip her hips, yanking her closer. The heat is unbearable, searing through the thin layers of fabric between us.

"You're infuriating," she pants against my lips, her fingers fumbling with the buttons of my shirt.

"And yet, here you are," I growl, nipping at her bottom lip before moving down, my mouth trailing along her jaw, her neck. She arches against me, a soft moan escaping as I push her dress up, exposing lace and bare skin.

I grip her thighs, my fingers digging into her soft flesh. "Say it again," I demand, dragging my tongue over the pulse racing in her throat.

"You're infuriating," she breathes, but her words have no venom now just raw, aching need.

My hands move without hesitation, shoving her panties aside as I press my fingers against her. She's already drenched, her body more than ready for me.

"Fuck, Candy," I groan, sliding a finger through her slickness, teasing her. "This all for me?"

She trembles beneath my touch, her hands flying to my belt, tugging at it with a desperation that matches my own. "Shut up and fuck me, Asher."

A dark, satisfied chuckle rumbles from my chest as I unbuckle my belt, yanking my zipper down in one swift motion. I free myself, my cock throbbing as I position it against her entrance.

Her eyes lock onto mine, wide and burning. "No more doubts?" she whispers, her voice softer now, vulnerable.

I grip her chin, forcing her gaze to stay on mine. "No more talking."

Then I thrust into her, burying myself deep in one rough stroke.

Candy cries out, her nails digging into my shoulders as she clenches around me, her body welcoming me home. I curse, my hands gripping her hips as I pull back and slam into her again, setting a brutal, punishing pace.

Her head falls back against the desk, her body arching, her moans echoing through my office. "Asher—"

"Say my name again," I demand, grinding against her, making her feel every inch of me.

Her fingers claw at my arms, her legs tightening around my waist. "Asher, please."

I lean over her, bracing myself with one hand on the desk while the other grips her thigh, hitching it higher. My lips find hers again, swallowing every sound she makes, tasting her desperation, her surrender.

She's mine.

Every gasp, every moan, every broken plea; it's all mine.

The desk shakes beneath us, the scattered papers long forgotten. All that exists now is Candy hot, breathless, and completely undone beneath me.

I can feel her body tightening, the way she trembles, the way her walls clench around me, pulling me deeper.

"Come for me," I order, my voice rough, desperate.

And when she does when she shatters beneath me, crying out my name like a prayer, I follow, letting go, my body pulsing deep inside her as I lose myself completely.

We stay there panting, locked together for what feels like an eternity, but in reality, it is only minutes.

What the hell have I done?

The weight of what just happened presses down on me, but I can't bring myself to move, to step away from her. She's still perched on the edge of my desk, her dress wrinkled, her lips swollen, and her eyes filled with too many emotions to decipher.

I should say something. I should fix this. But all I can think about is how she felt, how she responded to me, and how she shattered in my arms as if she belonged there.

But she doesn't.

Because I don't trust her.

And yet I can't seem to let her go.

I step back, zipping my pants back into place and tucking my hands in my pockets. "This doesn't change anything, Candy."

She exhales sharply, running a hand through her tangled hair. "I can't believe you," she whispers, her voice shaking not with fear, but with frustration, with hurt. "You think so little of me that you'd rather believe I betrayed you than accept the truth."

I clench my jaw, my hands fisting at my sides. "The truth? You mean the truth you conveniently decided to tell me after running to him?"

Her eyes blaze. "I wasn't running to him. I was breaking down, Asher! And he was there. That's it. But you—" She laughs bitterly, shaking her head. "You'd rather believe I was in his bed than believe I'm carrying your child."

Something inside me twists, sharp and merciless. "Because I know what Torin is capable of," I snap. "I've seen it before. I won't be the fool again."

She pushes off the desk, shoving at my chest with both hands. "You already are! You're the fool, Asher. Because you're pushing me away. You're letting your past dictate your future, and you're too damn blind to see what's right in front of you."

My body locks up. She's too close, her scent still clinging to my skin, her words cutting deeper than I want to admit.

Then she steps back. Straightens her dress. Smooths her hair. And when she looks at me again, something inside her has shifted.

Resolve.

Determination.

Resignation.

My stomach drops.

"I'm done fighting you," she says quietly. "Believe what you want. Hate me if it makes it easier for you. But this baby?" She places a protective hand over her stomach. "They're real. And whether you like it or not, you will be a father."

She turns on her heel, marching toward the door.

Panic grips me, primal and uncontrollable.

I should stop her.

I should say something.

But I stand here, watching her walk away, my chest tightening with something dangerously close to regret.

Because deep down, I know the truth.

I've already lost her.

And this time, it's my fault.

Chapter Seventeen

Candy

I don't cry when I leave the building. I don't cry in the elevator, or when I hand over my badge, or even when I walk past the coffee cart that always gets my name wrong. It's not until I'm three blocks away, standing on a slushy curb with a suitcase handle digging into my palm and the freezing wind needling my cheeks, that the tears finally come. Not dramatic ones either. Just quiet, ugly, soul-deep tears that burn more than they fall. I pull my beanie lower, as if I hide behind wool and shame, no one will see the way my whole world just cracked apart at the seams. I should've known better. Should've kept my distance. Should've kept my heart locked up tighter than Fort Knox instead of handing it over to a man like Asher Monroe. A man who sees everything in terms of value, cost, and return on investment.

Apparently, I wasn't worth the risk.

My phone buzzes in my pocket, but I don't look. I already deleted his contact. I don't need to see his name to know that if he's texting me now, it's not because he suddenly believes me.

It's because he's trying to manage fallout. That's what I was to him in the end. A complication. An HR nightmare. Something to clean up.

I'd been so stupid. I thought he saw me. Not just my work ethic or the way I organized his schedule down to the second, but me. The girl who stayed late to chase dreams she could barely afford. The one who made jokes under her breath to make him smile. The one who, just once, wanted to be more than convenient. But when it mattered, he looked at me like I'd betrayed him. Like I'd manipulated him. As if I were just another problem to solve, not a person to love.

The Uber driver barely says a word when I slide into the back seat, which is perfect because I don't have anything left to say anyway. Not about New York. Not about the job I worked my ass off to get. Not about the man who made me feel like I was finally seen until he looked through me like I was disposable. We reach the terminal, and I buy a bus ticket with shaking hands, nearly dropping my card in the process. The attendant doesn't ask questions, just hands me a receipt and points me toward Gate 12.

I've never felt more alone.

It's a six-hour ride. I wedge myself into a window seat and pull my coat tight around my stomach. A guy is coughing behind me, a baby wailing somewhere in the back, and the smell of stale pretzels and sweat hangs heavy in the air. It's miserable. Perfect, really. I don't sleep. I just stare out the window as the city gives way to quiet suburbs and long stretches of dark highway. The farther we get from Manhattan, the more the ache in my chest settles into something solid.

His voice won't stop echoing in my head. "You should've told me."

"I don't like surprises."

"I thought I could trust you."

Each one cuts deeper than the last. I feel like a damn fool not just for sleeping with my boss, but for letting myself believe I was anything more than a holiday fling. How did I not see this coming? I should've. There were signs of hesitation in his eyes, the way he'd pull back just when I thought he was letting me in. The way he questioned me made me feel like a liability. He once told me that business is about instincts. That his gut never lied.

Well, mine did. Mine said he was safe.

When the bus finally rolls into Goshen, Connecticut, it's almost midnight. The town is silent under a fresh blanket of snow, as if someone hit pause on the world. I haul my suitcase down Main Street, the wheels squeaking over packed slush as I head toward the only place I have left. The house is still the same low-slung ranch I remember: weathered gray siding, a porch wrapped in string lights that are half-burned out, and a rusted wind chime clinking lazily in the breeze. There's a dusting of snow on the old garden boots by the door, and the faint smell of firewood in the air. One of the barn lights is still on, casting a warm glow over the snow-covered fence.

I drag my suitcase up the porch steps and knock, heart thudding like it might give out. The porch light flicks on. My mom opens the door in her Christmas pajamas and a thick cardigan that's more patch than yarn at this point. "Candy? Baby girl, what...?"

I break. Right there. Fall into her arms like I'm sixteen again and just flunked my calculus final. Her arms wrap tight around me, and I breathe in the scent of vanilla lotion and cinnamon tea. For the first time in too long, I let someone hold me without fear of breaking apart completely.

She guides me inside, kicking the door shut with her foot. "You're freezing. Sit down. I'll make cocoa."

I drop into the old recliner by the fire, hands still shaking, boots still wet with slush. She moves around the kitchen with practiced ease, grabbing a pot, heating milk, stirring in cocoa powder and cinnamon.

The scent hits me before the warmth does. She hands me a steaming mug and crouches beside me. "You want to tell me what happened?"

I swallow hard. My lips barely move. "I'm pregnant."

She doesn't flinch. Just puts her hand on my knee. "Do you want to talk about him?"

I shake my head. "He didn't believe me. Thought I was trying to trap him or something."

She doesn't say anything for a long moment. Then softly, "You always see the best in people. Even when they don't deserve it."

I sip the cocoa and let her sit beside me on the floor until my breathing evens out.

The next morning, I wake up in my old bedroom, surrounded by faded posters, chipped white furniture, and the soft creak of baseboard heat. My suitcase sits in the corner, unopened. It feels strange being here, like slipping into an old coat you forgot you owned. Familiar, but a little too tight in the shoulders.

Mom made waffles. Of course she did. She sets a plate in front of me and pours syrup with a smile that wobbles at the edges. "You want to talk about it?"

I shake my head. Not yet. Maybe not ever.

She doesn't push. Just squeezes my hand and says, "You don't have to figure it all out today. You're safe. That's enough for now."

I nod, throat too tight for words, and dig into the waffles. They're slightly burned on the edges and way too fluffy in the middle, but I swear they taste like forgiveness.

After breakfast, I help her wash dishes. Neither of us says much. She hums along to the radio one of those old crooner Christmas stations that only plays songs from before 1970.

When the last plate is dry and the counter wiped down, she nudges me toward the living room. "Go rest. I'll put on the kettle and find that peppermint tea you love."

I sink into the couch with a blanket wrapped around me, and for the first time in days, I let myself be still. Not productive. Not planning. Just still. The quiet settles deep in my bones, and I realize how long it's been since I felt anything close to peace.

It's not a solution. Not yet. But it's a start.

Chapter Eighteen

Asher

Candy hasn't shown up in three days.

At first, I thought she was just cooling off. Taking a day. Maybe two. The kind of silent protest that still ends with her back at her desk, muttering under her breath while she updates my calendar. She's that kind of person stubborn, yes, but reliable. Blizzards, stomach flu, surprise board meetings, she always showed up. Hell, I half expected her to walk in Monday morning like nothing happened, make a snarky comment about my tie, and pretend we didn't detonate everything between us in the middle of my office.

But she didn't.

And now her absence is loud. Obvious. Carved into every corner of this place.

But by nine-thirty, I've checked my phone four times. By ten, I've refreshed my inbox at least a dozen times. There's no unread message. No cheeky Post-it left on my monitor. Just absence. Loud and sharp.

I walk by her desk twice. Her chair's tucked in. Her holiday mug sits in the corner, cold and empty. I open her top drawer. Pens. Color-coded sticky notes. The lip balm she always forgot to put away. Everything untouched. Everything hers. And not.

By noon, I can't take it anymore. I leave my floor and take the stairs down to the accounting department. Serina's office is tucked in the corner, humming with fluorescent lighting and the soft clatter of keystrokes filling in spreadsheets.

She glances up when I knock lightly and step in. "Didn't expect to see you down here."

I ignore the comment. "Have you heard from Candy?"

Serina closes her laptop slowly. "Yes."

I wait. But she doesn't elaborate.

"Is she okay?" I ask.

She sighs and leans back in her chair. "That's not for me to say."

"Serina, please. I just... I need to know if she's alright."

Her eyes soften for a split second before she schools her features. "You should talk to Maxine."

"Serina—"

"I'm not in HR, Asher. She's my friend. And she's hurting. Talk to Maxine." I press my lips together and nod once.

HR is on the other side of the building, tucked behind Legal. It takes everything in me not to storm through the hallway.

When I reach Maxine's office, the HR director looks up from her screen, peering over her glasses with the same composed disapproval she reserves for corporate misconduct.

"Can I help you, Mr. Monroe?"

"I need to know if Candy Hart submitted a resignation."

Maxine doesn't flinch. She clicks a few keys and pulls up a screen. "Yes. Effective immediately. Submitted three days ago. Her employee file has been updated to reflect voluntary separation."

"Did she give a reason?"

Maxine pauses. "Personal."

"Can you give me her address?"

"You know I can't do that."

I exhale, dragging a hand down my face. "Please. Just... off the record. I need to check on her."

She considers me, then rises and closes the office door. Her expression softens just enough. "She didn't list a new address. Just that she was returning to family."

I nod, jaw tight. "Was it was it because of what I said?"

Maxine raises an eyebrow. "I'm not a therapist, Mr. Monroe. But I would suggest reflecting on how your actions impacted one of the best employees this company has had in years."

She slides a sticky note across the desk. "This is her last known address. I suggest you use it wisely."

Back home, I try to text her. Again. Draft. Delete. Rewrite. Delete. Nothing I say feels right. Too little. Too late.

I go to the closet. Her scarf is still there. Burgundy. Soft. Still smells like peppermint and her shampoo. I hold it like it's fragile. Like if I close my eyes hard enough, I'll open them and find her standing in the doorway, rolling her eyes at me.

But she's not.

I sit down on the floor and pull out the drawer from my nightstand. Inside is a receipt from the charity auction night, an absurd number handwritten in red ink across the top. Thirty-five thousand for one date. One night. The start of everything and the beginning of the end.

I try to go to bed.

The sheets still smell like her peppermint and vanilla, and something softer I could never name but always noticed when she leaned over to hand me a file or whisper a reminder.

It hits like a gut punch.

I sit down on the edge of the mattress, fingers digging into the sheets, willing the scent to disappear. Willing her to be here instead.

The pillow has a faint smudge of mascara. I don't even know when she left it. Probably one of the nights she stayed late, curled into my side, falling asleep before the late news ended. She always said she hated sleeping in makeup. But she stayed anyway. With me. Trusted me.

And what did I do?

I drove her out of the city with a few careless words and a look that said she wasn't enough. A look I know she saw because it's burned into my memory now, playing on a loop every time I blink.

I lie back and stare at the ceiling. The silence is brutal. No quiet breathing beside me. No warmth curled against my side. Just the heavy press of what I lost.

I roll over and reach for her side of the bed, but it's cold. I drag the pillow to my chest, but it feels like mockery. This bed was ours. For a moment. For one small, perfect sliver of time where we weren't boss and assistant, or two people caught in the middle of something complicated. Just two people trying to make room for something good.

But now it feels wrong.

Too big. Too empty.

I rip the sheets off tearing the comforter back, wrenching the pillows off the bed and shoving them in the corner like it'll erase her. Like I won't still wake up reaching for her out of habit.

Like I didn't break the only person who made this place feel like home.

I stand there, chest heaving, heart pounding against my ribs like it's trying to outrun the shame bleeding into every crack in my chest. My fists clench around the edge of the mattress until my knuckles turn white.

Then I turn and walk out. Sleep isn't coming.

Not in this bed.

Not in this life I built so carefully only to find it meant nothing without her in it.

By midnight, I'm back at the office. I don't turn on the lights. Her desk is just as she left it: monitor off, a mug still in the corner, a sticky note pad with little doodles along the side.

There's a note under the keyboard tray: Don't forget to buy more tea. And smile. You're not as scary when you smile.

My heart caves in on itself. I sink into her chair. Grip the arms. Try to steady myself.

I sit in her chair, elbows on my knees, head in my hands.

She used to sit here every morning with a mug of peppermint tea and a quiet hum under her breath. Never loud. Just enough to remind me the world wasn't all deadlines and decimal points. And I ruined that. I see her everywhere; in the half-scribbled sticky notes, the empty mug in the corner, the perfectly arranged desk drawer she always pretended wasn't color-coded.

God, I miss her. Not just the way she kept the office together. Her. The way she looked at me was like I wasn't just a name on the building. The way she smiled, even when I didn't deserve it.

And now?

Now she's gone. Because I made her believe she wasn't wanted. Not the baby. Not her. And the worst part? She believed it without question. I scroll through old security footage watch her smile at the receptionist, pass Serina a candy cane, hum along to the holiday music under her breath. I turn the volume up just to hear her voice again.

Then I check her sent emails. The last one she sent before quitting was to the facilities department. A thank-you for fixing the heater under her desk. Before that, she sent me my schedule for the week, highlighted in green, with her notes in the margins.

I open a blank message.

Come back.

I need you.

I'm sorry.

I don't send it. Just leave the cursor blinking. Empty.

She was magic, and I didn't see it until she was gone. I made her feel disposable. And if she never comes back, I'll live with that. But if there's a chance any chance I can make it right, I'll take it. Because Candy Hart was never just a complication. She was the best thing that ever happened to me.

And I damn well intend to prove it.

Chapter Nineteen

Candy

Home doesn't feel like home. Not really.

I curl my legs beneath me on Mama's old floral couch, a quilt wrapped tight around my shoulders like armor. Outside the frost-covered windows, Goshen looks precisely the same as I left it: sleepy, slow, stitched with porch lights and pine trees. The kind of town where time forgets to move.

The couch dips as Mama sits beside me and presses a mug of peppermint tea into my hands. The scent alone makes my throat close.

"You sure you don't want to call him?" she asks gently.

I shake my head. "He made it pretty clear what he thought."

She sighs, brushing a curl from my forehead like I'm six again. "You always were the brave one. But even brave girls need help sometimes."

Help. It's such a small word for everything I've avoided asking for.

"You're home now," she said. "Whatever happened, you're home. You know you can stay as long as you want."

"I know."

She squeezes my hand. "You're not a burden, baby. You're my girl. And we're gonna figure this out."

The kindness nearly undoes me. My eyes sting, but I blink fast, unwilling to fall apart again. Not here. Not in front of her. She's held me together too many times already.

I press the mug to my lips to hide the wobble in my chin and let the warmth of the tea anchor me. The peppermint steam curls up into my face, grounding me.

It's Christmas Eve tomorrow. And I should be in the city, balancing spreadsheets, fixing last-minute issues, rolling my eyes as Asher forgets again that his signature is required in blue ink, not black. I should be moving through my color-coded planner like always, my entire day mapped out in fifteen-minute increments.

Instead, I'm here. Wrapped in a blanket I've had since high school, drinking tea like it's medicine, and pretending I'm not drowning.

And he hasn't called. Hasn't texted. Hasn't come after me.

Maybe that's answer enough.

"I left without telling anyone but Serina," I murmur. "Just packed and left."

Mama smooths the edge of the quilt. "Sometimes protecting your peace looks a lot like running. Doesn't mean it was the wrong thing to do."

"I didn't even give him a chance to fix it."

She hums. "Would he have?"

I think about the way his face changed when I told him. The distance. The cold disbelief. The way he looked through me instead of at me.

"No," I whisper. "He wouldn't."

Mama lets the silence stretch, long and thoughtful. The wind whistles past the window, and somewhere down the street I hear kids laughing, the clatter of ladders, the soft curse of tangled lights. A dog barks twice, sharp and excited. Somewhere, someone plays Christmas music too loud on a porch radio.

"You want to tell me about the baby?" she asks after a while.

I swallow. "It's early. Still the first trimester. I haven't seen a doctor yet. Just the test. But it was positive."

Her hand wraps around mine again. "We'll find a clinic in town after Christmas. You're not alone in this, Candy girl. Not ever."

I nod, but my chest aches. I feel like I've let her down. Like I've disappointed everyone.

Mama doesn't let go. "You know," she says softly, "when you were seven, you used to line up your stuffed animals and make them pretend to answer phones and take notes. Said you were running your own office. Even gave them names. Miss Bunny was your receptionist. I always knew you'd leave here and make something big of yourself."

I laugh, startled by the memory. "Miss Bunny was underqualified and always late."

"She was a stuffed rabbit, Candy."

"Exactly."

We fall into easy laughter, the first real one I've had in days. And then I reach for my planner. It's battered and almost empty now, the pages curling at the edges. I flip past the color-coded tabs, the lists of meetings and appointments and supply orders. All of it is obsolete.

I find a blank page and start a new list.

Things I Can Control:

What I eat.

Where I go.

How I spend my time.

Things I Can Fix:

My résumé.

My confidence.

My expectations.

Things Worth Showing Up For:

My baby.

Me.

The list is short. Uneven. A little raw. But it's something. A thread I can hold on to when everything else feels like it's slipping through my fingers.

"You always did love your lists," Mama says, smiling gently over the rim of her tea.

"They make things feel manageable."

Just then, the front door creaks open. A gust of cold air sweeps in along with the familiar sound of heavy work boots on hardwood.

"That wind's biting out there," my dad calls from the entryway, his voice warm and rough like gravel. "Smells like someone made tea."

Mama raises her eyebrows at me. "You want to tell him, or should I?"

I hesitate, my heart kicking. "I'll tell him," I say, quieter than before but a little more sure.

She gives my hand a gentle squeeze and stands. "I'll get him settled. Give you a minute."

I nod, watching her move toward the hallway as my dad's voice rumbles closer.

"We're gonna be okay," she says again, glancing back at me. "All of us."

And for the first time in days, I almost believe that.

My dad's sitting at the kitchen table, sipping from a chipped blue mug and flipping through the local paper when I join him. He looks up, takes one look at my face, and sets the mug down with a decisive thud.

"What happened?" he asks, voice low and steady.

I pull out the chair across from him and sit down, bracing myself. "I'm pregnant."

He doesn't say anything at first. Just blinks. Then he leans back slowly, folding his arms across his chest.

"Is it that city man's?"

I nod.

His jaw works. "I'm gonna kill him."

"Dad "

"No, Candy. You don't treat someone like that. Especially not my daughter." He stands like he means to grab his coat and go find Asher right now, but I catch his sleeve.

"Dad, please. I don't need you to fight him. I need you to be here. For me. For the baby."

He stares down at me, nostrils flaring, then sighs and scrubs a hand over his face. "Damn fool," he mutters. "You give a man a chance to be something, and he throws it away."

I nod once. That part, at least, we agree on.

He turns on his heel and stalks out the back door. I hear the barn doors groan open a minute later, then the shuffle of wood on wood, something dragging across the floor.

When he returns, he's carrying a dusty, dented cradle. My old one. And behind him, Mama trails in with a box of baby clothes.

"If that no-good city man can't be a man," my dad grunts, setting the cradle down in the hallway, "then I'm gonna make damn sure my daughter doesn't want for a single thing."

Mama sets the box down beside it and presses a kiss to my temple. "Let's go to town tomorrow," she says. "Start fresh. New things. New chapter."

I nod, my throat too tight for words.

Later that night, after the house quiets and the peppermint tea is long gone, I bundle up and step outside. The night is crisp and quiet, the stars clear and bright.

I walk down to the lake where I used to skate as a kid. The surface is frozen solid, the moonlight making it look like glass. I sit on the old bench nearby and press my hands to my belly.

"I don't know what the future looks like," I whisper to the growing life inside me. "But I promise I'll try. I'll be someone you can count on."

My voice catches on the wind, but I don't stop. I stay there until the cold numbs everything but the fire in my chest, and for the first time, I let myself hope that maybe, just maybe, I can build something new from everything that's broken.

Chapter Twenty

Asher

I don't know what I expected when I pulled up to the address Maxine gave me, but it wasn't this.

The house is small. Faded green siding. A cracked driveway that's half covered in snow. There's a busted tricycle leaning against the porch railing and a dented mailbox that tilts to one side like it's just as tired of standing as I am.

It's not what I pictured for Candy. Not even close.

I kill the engine and just sit there, the defrost humming low, trying to figure out what the hell I'm even doing. She's gone. Packed up her whole life and disappeared like I never meant anything. But that's not true, is it? I did mean something. She just didn't believe it.

And maybe that's my fault.

The landlord answers on the second knock. Middle-aged, grumpy, and already annoyed that I've interrupted his evening. He squints up at me like he knows exactly what kind of man I am and doesn't like it one bit.

"You looking for Candy?"

I nod. "I'm her—" What? Boss? Not anymore. "I'm trying to find her."

"She's not here. Cleared out a couple of days ago. Paid up through the end of the month, boxed up her stuff, and left. Didn't say much. Said she'd set up forwarding with the post office."

My stomach sinks. "Do you know where she went?"

"Didn't say. Just that it was out of state."

Out of state.

"She leave anything behind?"

He eyes me warily, then shrugs. "A couple of kitchen things and some junk furniture. If you want to see the place, I haven't cleaned it out yet."

I follow him up the creaking steps and into the apartment. It's cold, and the heat has already shut off. The scent of old wood and cheap cleaner clings to the air. There's a narrow galley kitchen to the left, chipped countertops, and a flickering overhead light. The living room is barely big enough for a couch; she must've used a sagging thrift-store piece left behind like a ghost.

The walls are bare. No photos. No color. Just a hollow space where a life used to be.

I step into what was probably her bedroom. A small mattress still sits on the floor, stripped down to the bare sheet. The window is cracked open a half inch, letting in icy air and a soft whistle of wind.

She lived here? Candy, bright, capable, organized Candy, called this place home?

I think of my penthouse. The polished floors. The view of the skyline. Heated towel racks and voice-controlled lights. And she came in every day, held herself together, handled everything I threw at her, and went home to this?

Guilt hits low and hard.

She never once asked for anything. Never complained. Never acted like she was owed more. And I, god, I saw her every damn day and never really saw her.

I run a hand through my hair and step back outside, boots crunching on the thin crust of ice on the porch. I take one last look at the apartment door, then get in my car.

Back at the office, everything feels off-kilter. Her desk is still empty. Her nameplate is still on the edge like she'll walk in any minute and start rattling off appointments and corrections. But she won't.

I try calling. Her phone goes straight to voicemail.

I call again.

And again.

Eventually, I stop pretending I'm not begging.

Please, Candy. Just tell me where you are. Let me fix it. Let me try.

But silence answers every time.

So I sit at my desk long after everyone else leaves. I stare at her empty chair and remember the sound of her laughter, the way she rolled her eyes when I was being difficult, the soft little smile she wore when she didn't think anyone was watching.

Eventually, I get up and walk to the sleek sideboard tucked near the corner; the one meant for client meetings and boardroom schmoozing, always stocked with top-shelf liquor no one touches during office hours.

Except tonight.

I pour two fingers of whiskey into a glass, then double it. It burns going down, and I welcome the sting. One drink turns into two. Then three. The quiet buzz in my head dulls the edge of guilt, but not enough.

The elevator dings.

I glance up, expecting the night janitor. Instead it's Torin. And he looks pissed.

"You got a second?" he asks, not waiting before stepping inside and letting the door close behind him.

"Not really in the mood for whatever this is."

He crosses his arms. "Tough. We're doing it anyway."

I scoff and pour another glass, waving it toward him. "Want one?"

He doesn't move. "You're drunk."

"Working on it."

Torin steps closer. "She called me. A few days ago. Said she quit. Said you gave her no choice."

My jaw clenches. "That's between me and Candy."

"No, it's not," he snaps. "You don't get to bulldoze through people and act like collateral damage doesn't count. She was the best damn thing that ever happened to you. And you let her walk."

"I didn't let her do anything. She left."

He narrows his eyes. "Because you broke her trust. You didn't just question her; you humiliated her."

I look away, jaw grinding. "I saw the two of you. Talking. Whispering. What the hell was I supposed to think?"

Torin goes still. "Is that what this is about?"

I down the rest of the whiskey. "It looked familiar. Too familiar."

He exhales sharply, understanding dawning. "This isn't about Candy. Not really. It's about Lila."

My stomach knots. "Don't."

"No," he growls. "You think I don't remember how that ended? How she told you it was me, how she used both of us to get ahead? I never touched her, Asher. I didn't betray you. She did."

I turn away, bracing my hands on the edge of the sideboard. "You don't get to rewrite history."

Torin walks around to face me. "I'm not rewriting anything. I'm telling you the truth. Again. Because apparently you didn't hear it the first time."

I stare at him, breathing hard. "And what if I was wrong?"

"Then you owe Candy a hell of a lot more than silence."

He backs away, his voice lower now. "She didn't deserve what you gave her. She didn't ruin anything. You did."

I close my eyes as he walks out, his words slamming into every nerve.

And I know he's right.

I open my laptop and start searching for private investigators. I don't know what I'm looking for. I don't even know where to start. But the idea of doing nothing makes my skin crawl.

I scroll through listings, reading reviews, clicking through websites. Everything feels shady or over-the-top. Like hiring someone would cross a line I'm not ready for.

But if it means finding her? Finding them?

I keep searching, clicking through page after page of private investigators, even as the whiskey turns warm in my veins and the office lights hum low around me. I jot down notes on a pad I don't remember grabbing, star names that might be worth calling, highlight numbers even though I haven't worked up the nerve to dial a single one yet. It feels desperate. Like grasping in the dark. But it's more than I was doing before.

It's a long shot.

But it's something.

Eventually, I close the laptop and sit back with a heavy exhale, my hand dragging down my face as I let the silence wrap around me like a sentence.

I don't care how long this takes. I don't care how far she's gone.

I'm going to find her.

And this time, I'm not letting her go.

Not again.

Not ever.

Chapter Twenty-One

Candy

It's Christmas Eve.

Snowflakes swirl outside the kitchen window, tiny white whispers against the glass, and I press my hand to the warm ceramic of the tea mug, pretending it's enough to settle the ache in my chest. Mama's still in her robe, humming along with the old Nat King Cole record spinning in the corner. There's something achingly familiar about it all. The clink of the spoon against the sugar bowl. The smell of cinnamon and clove steeping in her mug. It feels like the kind of moment I used to dream about on cold nights in the city when everything was too loud, too fast, too hard.

And still, my insides twist with unease.

I haven't told her yet. Not everything. She knows about the baby, knows I left, knows I'm here. But not what happened after. Not the way Asher looked at me like I'd betrayed him somehow. Like I'd let him down. I keep replaying it, hoping to find the version where he doesn't flinch. Where he says some-thing—anything—that doesn't hollow me out from the inside.

Mama sets a plate of toast in front of me, the kind she always used to make when I was sick—buttered and cut diagonally. "You keeping anything down yet?"

"Trying to."

She gives me a look that says she knows I'm dodging the issue. But she doesn't push. She just sits across from me, wrapping her hands around her mug like it's the only thing anchoring her.

It's been quiet for a long time. Just the soft hum of the record, the hiss of the radiator, the wind tapping like a secret against the window.

And then the back door creaks open.

Daddy steps into the kitchen, boots tracking snow across the mat. He shrugs out of his jacket, hangs it on the hook, and pauses when he sees me. His eyes flick to Mama, then back to me, softer now.

"You eatin'?" he asks.

I nod.

"Good."

He pours himself some coffee and settles into his usual chair at the head of the table. But he doesn't reach for the newspaper or start talking about the weather. He just watches me over the rim of his mug like he's trying to solve a puzzle with too many missing pieces.

"I ran into Ms. Hendricks in town yesterday," he says after a minute. "Asked about you. Said folks heard you were back."

I tense. "What did you tell her?"

"My daughter came home for Christmas. That's all anyone needs to know."

Relief loosens something in my chest. "Thanks."

He nods, slow and sure. Then he sets his mug down with a soft thud. "You know you don't have to carry it all by yourself."

"I know."

"You don't have to tell us everything right now either. Just... don't lock it all up inside."

I nod again, throat thick. "It's just hard to talk about."

He leans back, eyes still on mine. "You ever gonna tell us what happened with him?"

I hesitate. Then I nod slowly. "He thought I lied to him. About the baby. About everything. And instead of listening, he just shut down. Said things I can't forget."

Daddy's mouth flattens into a hard line. "He yell at you?"

"No. Not like that. He just... stopped seeing me. I wasn't a person anymore. Just a problem to solve. Or avoid."

He exhales sharply through his nose. "Sounds like a man too used to power and not enough to people."

"I think he was scared," I say quietly. "He saw me talking to someone he doesn't trust, and it brought up stuff from his past. It doesn't excuse it. But maybe it explains some of it."

Daddy rubs a hand over his jaw, his expression still tight. "So you still think there's something worth saving there?"

I look down at my toast. "I don't know. I just know I loved him. And I don't stop loving people easily."

He pushes back his chair and stands, his face softening as he reaches out and squeezes my shoulder. "Well. Until he comes around and proves he's worth that kind of love, we've got work to do."

I glance up, surprised. "Work?"

He jerks a thumb toward the back door. "Baby furniture's all cleaned up and drying out in the barn. I already set up the changing table in the den, and I figure we can bring in the crib tomorrow. Your mama's been disinfecting everything like we're expecting royalty."

Tears prick at the backs of my eyes. "You didn't have to "

"Didn't have to. Wanted to. This is my grandbaby. And you're still my little girl."

He ruffles my hair before stepping toward the door again. "And don't worry about what people say. Let 'em talk. They'll still be talking when that baby's taking its first steps, and by then, you won't care."

The door shuts softly behind him this time.

I wipe at my eyes and look across the table at Mama. She's smiling, eyes glassy.

"He's been out there all morning, makin' sure that mobile still turns," she whispers.

I laugh softly, then stand and pull my planner from the counter. I flip past the busy, color-coded pages of what my life used to be and find a blank space.

Christmas Eve List

Things I Can't Change:

What he said.

How it ended.

The past.

Things I Can Do:

See a doctor.

Build a future.

Buy peppermint ice cream even if it's snowing.

Things I Know for Sure:

This baby deserves love.

I'm stronger than I feel.

I'm not alone.

I stare down at the list I've just written, the ink soft and steady on the page, each word anchoring me a little more firmly to the present. It isn't some dramatic revelation or a sweeping sense of clarity it's quieter than that. Like the soft hush of snow outside the window, like a breath I didn't know I'd been holding, finally letting go.

And for the first time in days, it doesn't feel like I'm unraveling.

It doesn't feel like the end.

It feels like the start of something else—something new and fragile, but mine.

I wrap my fingers more tightly around the warm mug and let myself breathe. Just breathe. The peppermint steam curls around my face like a balm, and I lean into it, grounding myself in the scent, in the sound of Nat King Cole still drifting through the house, in the weight of my mama's quiet strength and my daddy's unexpected tenderness.

I don't have a plan. Everything still feels like a shattered compass spinning in too many directions, and I have no idea where I'm going or how I'll get there. All I have is this kitchen, this list, and the steady thrum of something like hope beginning to retake root.

But I'm not alone.

And today, that feels like enough to keep going.

Chapter Twenty-Two

Asher

New Year's Eve used to mean something. Champagne toasts, investors in tuxedos, noise spilling out of every corner of the city while the skyline shimmered like money and promise. I used to love it, the clean certainty of an ending that gave you permission to start over. A calendar flipping, a slate wiped clean.

Tonight it just feels like punishment.

The city outside my window is all sound and color, horns blaring and fireworks already cracking over the river. People lean out of windows with plastic cups raised high, already drunk on optimism. Inside my penthouse, it's nothing but dim light and silence. The expensive kind. The kind that presses in on you when there's nothing left to distract you from yourself.

The sideboard across the room gleams in the city's glow. It's meant for clients, for deals closed, for celebrations that come with contracts and handshakes. I've opened it three times tonight and poured drinks I don't really want. The glass in my hand isn't a celebration.

It's surrender.

I swirl what's left of the scotch and try not to think about how I got here. About how easily I ruined everything that mattered. How she stood in my office doorway, hands clenched at her sides, voice shaking but steady enough to break me. And instead of listening, instead of trusting the woman who had never once given me a reason not to, I went cold.

The clock on the stove reads 9:42 p.m.

Three hours until the new year.

Everyone else in this city is counting down to something.

I'm counting backward, retracing every misstep like it might lead me somewhere else if I stare at it long enough.

I don't need to leave to know where she isn't.

I can still see it when I close my eyes. Not in detail, not like a place I'm standing inside again, but in fragments that won't let go. The cracked steps. The cold air. The way her life looked when I finally bothered to notice it. How small the space was. How quietly she must have carried herself through my world every day, holding everything together, then gone home to a place that never asked anything of her except resilience.

I thought I was protecting myself.

What I was really doing was punishing her for someone else's sins.

That realization settles heavily in my chest, ugly and unavoidable. I've spent years telling myself I learned my lesson. That I was smarter now. More careful. That what happened with Lila was an anomaly, a betrayal I survived and buried and moved past.

That's the lie.

I didn't move past it. I built my life around it.

Control. Distance. Certainty. I made rules, systems, and schedules that kept everything neat and manageable. I trusted data, outcomes, and appearances because people were messy and unpredictable and capable of wrecking you when you let them get close enough.

Candy never fit into that system.

She was steady without being rigid. Capable without needing to dominate. She didn't demand space in my life; she simply occupied it quietly and competently until she mattered more than I was willing to admit. And when fear crept in, when something in me recognized the risk of that kind of closeness, I reached for the only weapon I knew.

Suspicion.

I tip the glass back and drain it, but it doesn't burn enough. The numbness isn't working tonight. Candy didn't lie. She didn't manipulate. She didn't angle for advantage. She didn't ask for anything she hadn't earned. She just wanted me to believe her.

And I didn't.

That truth sits heavier than the silence.

Fireworks boom outside, closer now. The noise fades again, leaving a strange, suspended quiet in its wake. I check the clock without meaning to. 11:17. Too much time left. Not enough. I flex my fingers around the glass, noticing how tight my grip is, how my knuckles ache like I've been bracing for impact.

I pace the length of the room, then turn and pace it again. My reflection follows me in the windows, fractured and doubled, a man who looks put together from a distance and hollow up close. I stop at the sideboard, reach for the bottle out of habit, then hesitate.

One more drink would make this easier.

It always does.

I set the bottle down untouched.

The idea of finding her twists something sharp in my chest. What if I do more harm than good? What if my showing up rips open something she's already worked to close? She didn't leave quietly by accident. She left because I made it impossible to stay.

Maybe the kinder thing would be to let her go.

The thought doesn't bring relief. It brings panic.

Because letting her go isn't kindness. It's cowardice dressed up as restraint. It's the same move I've made every time things get real. Withdraw. Control the damage. Walk away before I can be left.

That's the pattern.

And Candy paid for it.

I press my palms to the counter and bow my head, breathing through the tightness in my chest. I don't know if she'll want to see me. I don't know if she'll ever trust me again. I don't even know what I'll say when I find her.

But I know what I won't do.

I won't disappear.

 Not this time.

The clock ticks louder now. 11:58. Outside, voices rise in anticipation, the city holding its breath. I straighten, feeling the weight of the choice settle into place. This isn't about fixing everything. It's about facing what I broke without flinching.

Midnight comes in a rush of sound and light.

Cheers echo up the street, muffled and distant, like they belong to another life entirely. Midnight is coming whether I'm ready or not. I pace the length of the room, shoes whispering against polished floors, every reflection in the glass another version of me I don't like very much.

Control isn't safety.

It never was.

Safety is trust. And I broke it.

I stop at the counter and open my laptop. Not an email. Not an apology yet. Just a blank page and a blinking cursor that feels like a challenge. Like a line drawn in the sand between who I've been and who I have to become if I want any chance at fixing this.

Find Candy.

The words sit there, stark and simple. I don't know where she is. I don't know if she'll ever forgive me. I don't even know if she should.

But I know this. Doing nothing isn't an option anymore.

The clock flips to 12:00 a.m.

The city erupts. Light floods the windows. Somewhere far below, people kiss and laugh and make promises they hope will stick. I stand there in the glow of a brand-new year, feeling the weight of everything I've lost and everything I still might lose if I keep choosing fear over faith.

I close the laptop and rest my hands on the counter, breathing through the knot in my chest. I can't undo what I broke. I can't take back the things I said or the way I shut her out when she needed me most.

But I can stop pretending it didn't matter.

This isn't how our story ends.

Not if I'm finally willing to do the work.

Chapter
Twenty-Three

Candy

New Year's Day

The house wakes slowly, like it's stretching under a blanket of snow. Pipes hum, radiators sigh, and somewhere down the hall, the old clock clears its throat before deciding to chime. I lie still beneath Mama's quilt, the one with fading bluebells, and listen to the soft creak of the world coming back to life. Outside, everything is white and hushed; the kind of morning that looks like forgiveness.

For a while, I just lie there, tracing the pattern on the quilt and watching the frost catch in the corners of my window. The Christmas lights are still up on the porch, and Mama refuses to take them down until mid-January. She says the house looks too sad without them and that a bit of light never hurt anyone. Maybe that's why I've always loved Christmas—because it never demands perfection. It just shows up every year, gentle and forgiving, even when you don't feel worthy of celebration.

I slip into wool socks and Daddy's oversized navy sweater that smells faintly of cedar and smoke. The kitchen is warm, a single light over the sink painting the counter in gold. A folded note leans against the sugar jar in Mama's handwriting:

Went with your daddy to get eggs and the good bacon. Back soon. Cocoa on the stove.

I smile despite the ache behind my ribs. The cocoa waits, rich and dark, sending up peppermint steam. I wrap my hands around the mug, letting the warmth seep into me until the chill finally retreats. The faint scent of pine and nutmeg still lingers from Christmas morning though our tree's bare now except for a few stubborn strands of tinsel clinging to the branches. I make a mental note to help Mama take it down later, but part of me hopes she'll leave it just a little longer.

My phone sits on the windowsill, screen dark. I've avoided it for days, proud of my restraint. But the quiet is generous this morning, and I'm tired of flinching at ghosts. I pick it up. Notifications blink holiday sales, a message from Serina that says *thinking of you*, and one message that steals the air from my lungs.

The text is from last night, 11:53 p.m.

I'm sorry. I was wrong. I hope you're safe.

My thumb hovers, then falls away. I set the phone down face-first on the counter. I don't delete it. I don't respond. I just let it exist there, small and unfinished.

The back door opens with a groan. Daddy stomps snow from his boots, carrying grocery bags that rustle with promise. "Morning, kiddo," he says, his voice wrapped in warmth. Mama follows, cheeks pink, laughing as she shakes out her scarf.

"You sleep any?" she asks, reaching for a skillet.

"Some." I manage a smile. "Your note helped."

"Good. Cocoa's medicinal on January first."

Daddy sets down the bags. "And bread. Still warm from the bakery." The scent fills the kitchen—yeast, butter, and something like memory. "Figured we start the year right, fresh bread, collard greens, black-eyed peas–the works."

He's a man built of steady things: callused hands, quiet love, work done right the first time. When I told him about the baby, he didn't yell. He just went to the barn, started sanding my old crib, and hummed until Mama called him in for dinner. The next morning, he'd brought in half my childhood, repaired and ready.

"This tastes like a bribe," I say, taking a bite of bread. Butter melts over my tongue.

"Bribe, promise, same thing." He grins, then nods toward me. "You up for a drive later? There's a clinic open for holiday hours.

Your Mama sweet-talked them yesterday. They can see you if you're ready."

My hand goes to my stomach, instinct before thought. "Yeah," I whisper. "I'm ready."

The drive to Torrington is quiet and strangely beautiful. Snow clings to the edges of the trees, softening the world into something dreamlike. Daddy hums along to the radio an old Willie Nelson song, and Mama occasionally reaches over to squeeze my knee like she's reminding herself I'm real. I stare out the window, and my mind wanders over the past few weeks. The city feels far away now, like another lifetime. This silence isn't lonely; it's peace. And I didn't know how much I needed it until now.

Inside the clinic, tinsel still dangles from the counter, and a nurse in reindeer scrubs greets us with a smile that feels like a gift. The doctor is gentle, with a practical, kind tone. She asks if I want to hear the heartbeat.

I nod, breath trapped somewhere in my chest. The gel is cold, the wand colder. For a few seconds, there's nothing, just the hum of machines. Then a sound quick, steady, astonishing. My baby's heartbeat, tiny and sure.

Mama's hand finds mine, both of us laughing and crying at once. The doctor says, "Strong," and I believe her.

The sun is low when we drive home, gilding the snow in pink and gold. Mama insists on stopping for apples at the market and somehow comes out with panda slippers for me and a peppermint candle shaped like a tree. Daddy rolls his eyes but doesn't argue. By the time we reach the house, the windows glow with evening light, and smoke curls from the chimney like a sigh.

Daddy heads straight to the barn while Mama pulls out flour and sugar. "We'll make waffles tomorrow," she says, winking. "Seems fitting for a new beginning."

I help her set the table, the rhythm of it familiar and grounding—the clink of silverware, the hiss of the stove, the hum of the radio still playing Christmas standards. When Daddy finally comes in, his hands smell like cedar and polish. "Rocking chair's ready," he announces. "Looks better than new."

"You've been out there every day since she came home," Mama teases.

He shrugs. "Gotta make sure my grandbaby's got a proper start."

I don't say anything. Just smile through the burn in my throat.

Later, when the house is quiet again, I curl up on the couch beside the tree. The ornaments are packed away now, but the leftover strands of tinsel catch the light, spinning tiny constellations onto the ceiling. I open my planner to a blank page.

New Year's Day

Things I Know Now:

The heartbeat is real.

Fear doesn't shrink the future; it just crowds the view.

I can do hard things without punishment.

Things I Want to Remember:

Mama's hand in mine.

Daddy is waiting in the hall.

The sound that changed everything.

Things I Don't Have to Decide Today:

Forgiveness.

What to name a life.

Whether love gets another chance.

Things Worth Hoping For:

A soft place to land.

A reason to believe again.

Peace, however small.

The clock ticks steadily in the hall. Snowflakes drift past the window, lazy and endless. Somewhere upstairs, Mama hums a carol under her breath. I close my planner and whisper to the quiet, "This is a beginning."

And for the first time in weeks, it feels true.

Chapter Twenty-Four

Asher

The first morning back after New Year's always feels like someone turned the volume down on the city and up on the fluorescent lights. The elevator doors open to the executive floor and give me the same view as always—glass, steel, the skyline pretending to be a promise but the air's wrong. Too clean. It smells like lemon cleaner and absence.

Candy's desk hits me before my own office does. That empty chair is a blade. The nameplate looks temporary without her behind it, like a label on a box no one intends to open. There's a speck of glitter on the desktop—holiday shrapnel that somehow survived Facilities—and a faint peppermint wrapper crease on the corner of a notepad. It's ridiculous that I notice, but I do. It's more laughable that a random piece of trash and glitter could almost bring me to my knees.

"Happy New Year, Mr. Monroe." A voice from the hallway. Neutral, careful. People have learned to gauge the weather by me.

"And to you," I say, and make my mouth shape something that isn't a warning.

I unlock my door, drop my coat, and stand there long enough to count the breaths in my lungs. I didn't sleep much. When I closed my eyes, I saw peeling paint and a pink lamp left on a stairwell for a neighbor's child. I saw a mattress on the floor and a window that wouldn't close all the way. I saw the version of her life I never asked enough about. Every time I blinked, the accusations I threw at her came back with interest.

No more delay. I pick up the phone and call HR.

"Monroe," Maxine answers on the second ring, crisp and human at once. She's the only director who uses last names as both terms of endearment and warnings. "Back in the saddle already?"

"I need to talk," I say.

"I assumed," she says. "I have fifteen minutes before an exit interview. If you're asking for a miracle, make it ten."

"Your office," I tell her, and hang up before I start trying to make it sound more palatable than it is.

Maxine's space is what you'd expect if a spine had an office. Clean lines. A plant that thrives without fuss. Framed policies on the wall that make people sit up straighter without reading them. She doesn't offer me a chair. She knows I'll take one. I do.

"I'm aware Candy Hart resigned," I say, skipping the preamble. "But I need to make sure she has access to maternity coverage and any wellness resources we can legally provide."

Her expression doesn't flicker. Maxine doesn't hand out relief or disdain. She waits for them to come out of you. "She resigned voluntarily, effective immediately, which terminated benefits as of that date," she says. "You approved the separation in the system. I have your signature."

"I'm aware." The words taste like rust. "I'm also aware that there is an executive override window, within thirty days, for reinstatement in limited circumstances."

"There is," she says. "It's designed for administrative error or unavoidable interruption, not executive guilt."

I deserve that. I take it. "If she chooses not to return, she won't be required to," I tell her. "This isn't a coercion. I want the file reopened to reactivate coverage. Quietly. No press. No fanfare. No strings."

The arch of one eyebrow is so slight it may have been a trick of the light. "You understand reinstatement changes payroll, tax, and liability exposure, right? It also obligates the company to treat her as an employee, with all attendant rights."

"Yes," I say. "Treat her as an employee. With all attendant rights."

"You can't reinstate someone without their consent."

"I'm not asking to reinvent the law," I say. "I'm asking you to advise me on the path that gives her the most protection."

Silence settles, the kind that's full of the sound of someone counting to ten in their head. Maxine reaches for a folder and pulls out Candy's file. The tab with her name makes my throat go tight.

"Emergency contact?" I ask softly because this part feels like an intrusion I haven't earned.

Maxine doesn't look up. "Her mother," she says. "Goshen, Connecticut. The address was updated last year. We use it for payroll and tax forms, not for exes with good intentions."

"I'm not asking you to give it to me," I say quickly. "I want you to send a wellness packet there from HR. Resources. En-rollment information if she opts into reinstatement. A number that isn't mine."

Her gaze lifts to mine, searching, verifying, measuring the current against the man who sat in this chair a week ago and signed off on a resignation like it was a relief. "If we proceed," she says, "this is done by the book. Reinstatement paperwork goes out with clear language: no obligation to return, full benefits if she elects. We will include contacts for maternal health and legal support, as well as company-paid counseling referrals. No personal notes. No side channels."

"Good," I say. I mean it. "Thank you."

She closes the file. "This doesn't buy you absolution," she says, softer than I expect. "I know you know that. I want you to remember it."

"I do," I say. "I'm not trying to buy anything."

Her mouth eases at the corners. Not a smile. A ceasefire. She taps her keyboard, efficient as a metronome again. "I'll draft it. You'll approve. And, Monroe, if you ever try to use HR to fix what a direct apology should, I'll make a policy named after you."

That draws a breath out of me that might, on another day, have been a laugh. "Understood."

She stands; I stand. It's an old dance. At the door, she says, "And don't ask me for her address again."

"I won't," I tell her, and I mean that too.

On the accounting floor, the hallway smells like ink and last year's coffee. I shouldn't be down here; I'm the kind of executive who makes people pause their keystrokes when I appear. I go anyway.

Serina's office door is cracked. She's on the phone, brow furrowed, pen tapping against the margin of a spreadsheet. I wait in the hall until she hangs up. She sees me, startles, and recovers so fast it would be impressive if it didn't land like a reprimand.

"Mr. Monroe," she says. "We're closing Q4. If you're here to ask about variance reports, they're in your inbox."

"I'm here to apologize," I say.

Her pen stops tapping. "Oh."

I step inside, leave the door open, and take off the edge that makes people brace. "I put you in a spot you didn't deserve," I say. "No triangulating through you about Candy again. If you hear from her, you're not obligated to tell me. If you want HR support for anything I did that made your job harder, I'll back it."

Something in her posture loosens, like a wire cut carefully. "She didn't ask me to keep her secrets," Serina says, voice even. "But she didn't want to be the office rumor either."

"I made her the rumor," I say. Naming it makes my chest ache in a way that feels like repair. "I won't repeat the mistake."

"If you need anything from accounting that helps... the right way... ask me directly. I can't tell you where she is. But I can make sure her last expense report gets reimbursed today."

"Do it," I say. "And Serina thank you."

Her chin lifts. "Don't thank me yet. Just keep being the version of yourself who came in here."

I leave before I can ruin the progress by trying to narrate it into something larger than it is.

The rest of the morning, I do the uncomfortable work of cleaning up the mess she never let become my problem. I go through the calendar Candy built—her color-coding, her notes in the margins, the invisible scaffolding I only notice now because I leaned on it so hard I forgot it existed. I respond to emails she would have triaged with three keystrokes and a sticky note. I pick up the phone and make the call I'd usually let her make because I prefer to stay above the friction. The small humiliations feel right-sized. The day grows sharp edges I deserve to feel.

At 11:08, Maxine's draft hits my inbox. It's perfect—cold water and kindness in correct proportions. I add nothing. I sign and send it back. HR will print and mail the packet to the emergency contact address on file. Official. Proper. The opposite of a grand gesture. It feels like something a man who intends to be better would do.

I stare at my screen until the words blur. Then I push back from the desk and grab my coat.

There are more steps I can take that are mine to carry alone.

Jordan doesn't look surprised when I appear in his doorway. He never does; it's his curse and his gift. He waves me in, and after I shut the door behind me, he tips his chin at the chair across from him.

"You look less haunted," he says.

"I've asked HR to reinstate benefits. Wellness packet goes out today."

He whistles low. "Maxine let you do that?"

"She let the company do what was right," I say. "I'm trying to do my part without making it about me."

He steeples his fingers. "How's that going?"

"Like teaching a limb I've overused to rest," I say. "It wants to grab."

"Good," he says. "Not the grabbing, the noticing."

"I'm looking at private investigators," I tell him. "Not to chase. To confirm she's safe. If that's not possible, or if it crosses a line, I'll accept that. But if there's a way to get confirmation without violating her boundaries, I want it."

He studies me long enough to make sure the request isn't arrogance in a better suit. Then he nods once.

"Boundaries," he says. "Say them out loud before you hire anyone."

"I will."

"And, Asher?" he adds when I stand.

"Yes?"

"Whatever you write to her next, send the one that doesn't ask for a reply."

It's infuriating how much I need other people to say out loud the thing I already know. "Understood," I say, and pocket the card like a promise.

I don't call the PI from the office. I wait until I'm back in my condo, the sky outside moving toward early dark, the city a field of lit windows pretending to be stars. I stand at the glass, the phone against my ear, and listen as a line clicks open.

"Dean Hollis," a voice says. Calm. Professional. Not impressed by money. I like him immediately.

"This is Asher Monroe," I say. "Jordan Vance gave me your number."

He asks what I need. I tell him. No searches without consent. No surveillance. No contact. A single question: *Is she safe?* If the answer is no, tell me how to make yes happen without violating her boundaries. If the answer is yes, I don't ask any more questions.

He's quiet long enough that I think the call dropped. Then: "That's the first request I've had from a man in your position that didn't make me want to hang up," he says. "Give me twenty-four hours."

"Thank you," I say, and mean it like a prayer.

When the call ends, the condo is too quiet. I move because stillness feels like an old addiction. Coats go into the hall closet. The stack of donation receipts Candy set aside in a folder she wrote *sign if you want to be a person today* on a pink sticky note and drew a smiley face that irritated me precisely because it was true. I sign all of them now, not because I want to buy my way back into being decent, but because the organizations are good and because she saw something in me I'm not done trying to live up to.

The letter I wrote on New Year's is still open on my laptop, the one I emailed to myself so I wouldn't be tempted to sand it down. I print it and leave the pages on the counter. The words look like a man telling the truth, refusing to water them down. I don't add a single line. I print it.

Serina texts around seven: *Expense report processed. Also, accounting voted to order peppermint tea for the break room year-round. Consider it a tribute.*

I snort, and the sound surprises me. Approved, I reply. And thank you.

Before bed, I open my email and send a follow-up to HR, referencing the packet that went out earlier today. The subject line reads *Employee Support – Former EA.*

The body is simple: *Please confirm that Ms. Hart's packet includes clear instructions on reinstatement and a direct line to a counselor. If she contacts you, prioritize privacy and dignity. Do not inform me unless she authorizes it.*

I read it twice, then hit send.

I get into bed and lie there long enough to memorize the speed of the ceiling fan. At some point, sleep comes the way it always does when you finally stop forcing it.

Morning in the office brings a mostly clean inbox and a reply from Maxine confirming the packet is in the mail. It brings a calendar that looks empty without her color and a building that smells like hope and disinfectant. It brings a single text from a number I don't know until I do.

This is Hollis. She's safe. With family. No concerns at present. We did not contact her, per instruction.

I close my eyes and lean my forehead against the window. The glass is cold enough to shock me into my body. I let the relief come, and with it, the ache. Both belong.

There's work to do. There's a letter to deliver when, and only when, there's a way to do it that doesn't put her in the position of forgiving me to make me feel better. There's a company to run without asking anyone else to carry my consequences.

I straighten, pull my jacket on, and head for the door. When I pass her desk, I stop not to linger in the hurt, but to pick up the broken peppermint wrapper and drop it gently in the trash.

"New year," I say under my breath, not as a vow but as a direction. "Do it right."

Chapter Twenty-Five

Candy

The morning comes in thin bands of winter light, slow and pale across Mama's kitchen table. The peppermint candle she bought burns low, a soft pink tree melting into itself, and I tear off a tiny curl of wax just to have something to do with my hands. The house feels held by quiet, by coffee, by the way Mama hums when she thinks no one's listening.

On the porch, Daddy shakes salt onto the steps like he's blessing them. Every so often, he peeks in the window to make sure I'm eating the oatmeal he made. I spoon it up obediently. It tastes like cinnamon and love.

There's a stack of baby-name books on the counter now. Mama swears she doesn't remember putting them there. The covers are a little ridiculous—stars and moons and a baby wearing a knitted fox hat—but the sight of them makes something warm settle behind my ribs. I flip one open, then shut it just as fast. Not yet. It just feels too soon, too real, and entirely too big.

My phone vibrates once on the windowsill, skittering like a nervous bird. I don't move. It's probably another coupon; a subtle reminder that the world is still spinning without me. After a minute, the silence returns. Relief and disappointment tangle in my throat until I can't tell one from the other.

A knock sounds at the door. Not the back one, the front. We don't use that door much. My heart jumps into my throat, and my eyes meet Mama's across the kitchen.

I move to open the door but Daddy beats me to it. "Mornin'," I hear him say, followed by the polite voice he saves for strangers. "Yes, ma'am, she's here."

Mama and I stare at each other without saying a word. He brings a large white envelope to the table and sets it down as if it might bite him. The return address is a New York office tower printed in clean blue ink. Human Resources. The company letterhead I could recognize anywhere.

My stomach swoops to my knees.

"It's addressed to me," Mama says gently, sliding her readers on. "Emergency contact."

"Open it," I whisper, because I can't make my hands do it without shaking.

She breaks the seal with her thumbnail and reads, eyes moving steadily. Her mouth does a little surprised tilt that's not quite a smile. "It's... formal," she says. "But kind. Benefits information. Maternity coverage is available if you elect it. Counseling resources. A contact name who isn't... him."

I take the packet. The paper is thick, official. There's a cover note from Maxine, our HR director. She's the one who processed my hiring paperwork the woman with a spine of steel and a voice like a rulebook read aloud. I remember her shaking my hand on my first day and saying, *"Welcome to the circus. We keep it civilized most of the time."*

This sounds exactly like her precise, humane, no corporate spin. No *you have to.* No *we need you back.* Just: *you are entitled to these options if you want them. Here is how. Here is how to keep your privacy. Here is a direct line that will not loop to an executive.*

"He didn't write this," I say, skimming the page again. "Maxine wouldn't let him. But if it landed here, it's because she believed it mattered."

Mama sets her hand over mine, warm and steady. "Baby, I don't know what he asked for. I know what's in front of you. A choice."

Daddy snorts from the sink like he's refusing to be impressed on principle. "Choice is good," he says. "Just remember it's yours. Not his. Not theirs. Yours."

"Mine," I echo.

I tuck the packet beneath my planner and breathe through the prickle behind my eyes. It's not forgiveness. It's not even a conversation. It's a door propped open by a brick labeled *"We *will respect you.*" And somehow, that's enough to loosen the knot in my chest.

"Go get dressed," Mama says, too casually. "I promised Bernice we'd swing by the community center and help with donation sorting for the Winter Market."

"The Winter Market that is somehow still the Christmas Market until mid-January?" I tease because the town refuses to surrender to calendars when there are still snowmen on people's lawns.

"The very one." She winks. "Holiday spirit's like a stubborn stain. You just keep finding it."

I pull on leggings and a sweater that hides the soft new curve of me, then choose not to add the ridiculous panda slippers Mama bought. When I protest, she says shoes are a prison and life is short. I put on boots anyway but tuck the slippers in my bag for later.

The community center smells like old wood and lemon oil. Long tables are covered in everything from knitted scarves to little glass angels wrapped in tissue. Kids are painting signs for the raffle booth in the corner, smearing red and green letters onto cardboard. Someone presses a roll of tape and a stack of labels into my hands before I can protest.

"Put 'silent auction' on the craft baskets," Bernice instructs, moving at the speed of a well-meaning hurricane. "Oh, and take this note to Mary. She's in charge of well, you'll see."

Mary turns out to be a clipboard with a person attached to it. She hands me a list with a line item highlighted. I read it twice. *Supplies for waffle raffle covered.* The note in the margin reads *"anonymous sponsor."*

I stand there longer than I should, the letters blurring until they might say anything. It could be anyone. This town takes care of its own. People sponsor things all the time. It doesn't have to be him.

But I feel it anyway; the recognition like a bell struck low somewhere under my ribs.

I fold the list and tuck it into my back pocket like it's not essential. Like I'm not secretly clutching it.

When we finish labeling, Mama disappears into a conversation about napkin rings and whether glitter glue constitutes a biohazard. I wander toward the back, where volunteers are setting up the kitchen station card tables lined with waffle irons, batter prepped in easy to pour containers, coffee pots humming softly beside a mountain of syrup bottles. Mugs of hot chocolate stand at the ready. Someone has draped twinkle lights along the edge of the serving table, and there's a cardboard sign that says

CHRISTMAS WAFFLE STATION in letters that wobble like they're laughing at themselves.

I sit on a folding chair and pull out my planner.

January Third — Market Prep

Things I Can Control:

What I put in my body.

Where I spend my time.

What I say yes to.

Things I Can Consider (Later):

Benefits.

Counseling.

New job, near home, or back in the city.

Things I Don't Owe:

An immediate answer.

A performance of forgiveness.

Proof of pain.

If / When He Reaches Out Again:

Listen for listening.

No arguing about a past that already happened.

Ask for sustained gentleness, not grand gestures.

A little boy in a puffy blue coat wanders over and studies my list upside down. "Are you makin' waffles?"

"Eventually," I say solemnly. "But right now I'm making decisions."

He nods like that's the more impressive skill. "My mom says decisions are harder than algebra."

"Your mom is wise." I smile. "Want to help me put the lights in a less... dangerous configuration?"

We untangle as best we can. When we plug the lights back in, they glow steadily instead of in seizure-inducing flickers. The grin on his face is like we've solved a much larger problem than we have. Maybe he is right, maybe we have. Perhaps putting something to rights is a kind of miracle.

On the way home, the sky is filled with blues and pinks, which makes me wonder what the bundle growing inside me will be. Would Asher have wanted a son? The thought immediately turns bitter; the issue wasn't the pregnancy; it was me. I shake myself out of my funk when we stop at the store for milk and leave with a bag of clementines, a magazine with *New Beginnings!* splashed across the front in cheerful font, and a tin of cocoa we absolutely don't need. Mama blames marketing. I blame Mama.

Back at the house, Daddy's in the den again, tightening the last screws on the rocking chair he refinished earlier in the week. The crib's already set up in the corner of my room, soft lamplight spilling over the quilt Mama folded across its rail. He pretends not to notice me watching from the doorway.

"Didn't want the rocker squeakin' when the baby comes," he says gruffly, which makes precisely no sense given how far off that day still feels.

I hand him the tiny bag of nuts and bolts he's patting his pockets for and watch his hands work steady, sure, patient. He's always been good at putting things back together without making you feel foolish for breaking them in the first place.

"Bernice says supplies for the waffle raffle got covered," I say, too casually. "Anonymous."

He grunts which, in Daddy-speak, could be anything from *Good* to *Hmm*. After a minute: "There's more than one kind of apology. Money's the cheapest. Quiet help takes practice."

I think about the packet on the table. The way it didn't ask me for anything. The way it gave me everything I might need, even if I never go back.

"I don't know what to do yet," I admit.

"Then don't," he says, tightening a bolt with deliberate care. "Let tomorrow do some of the deciding for you."

After dinner, I shower and pull on the panda slippers because they make Mama clap, then curl into the corner of the couch with a blanket. The streetlight outside throws soft diamonds on the ceiling through the bare branches of the tree. My phone sits on the coffee table, screen black. I reach for it, then think better and go for the packet instead.

I read every page. Twice. I circle the counseling line and fold the edge down so I can find it with shaking hands if needed. When I finally put it away, I take out my journal the one with fresh paper and quiet promise and write a few lines to the baby.

Hi, little heartbeat. Today I learned a new thing about beginnings. They don't always feel like fireworks. Sometimes they're paperwork and waffles and the way your grandfather pretends he doesn't love pandas. Sometimes they're a letter that doesn't demand anything from you. I don't know what our life will look like yet. But I know this: I will choose us. I will choose peace whenever I can find it. And if someone wants to be in our lives, they'll have to choose peace too.

I close the journal and set it on the table. The house settles around me, old wood and new hope. In the kitchen, the peppermint candle sputters and goes out, a thin line of smoke curling like a ribbon before it fades.

I look at my phone one last time and let the quiet win. Not as punishment. As practice.

Tomorrow I'll call the clinic with follow-up questions. I might even fill out one of the forms in the packet and leave it stamped on the counter until I know whether to mail it.

Tonight I pull the blanket up to my chin and listen to the soft, steady clock in the hall. The sound isn't forgiveness or forgetting.

It's endurance. It's a promise that time can pass without breaking me.

And for now, that's enough.

Chapter Twenty-Six

Asher

It's strange waking up sober and not knowing what to do with the quiet.

The city outside my window hums like a thing alive, sirens, traffic, a thousand people trying to outrun themselves, but inside, it's still. Too still. The glass of water on the nightstand hasn't moved since I set it there last night. Neither have I.

I shower, shave, and stand in front of the mirror until the steam fades. The man who stares back isn't someone I recognize. Same suit. Same tie. Different eyes. There's no performance left to hide behind, no version of control that looks good in a boardroom. Just the consequences of a man who thought fear excused cruelty.

The HR packet went out. Maxine hasn't said anything else about it, and I didn't ask. Boundaries are the price of decency. I hope it made it to Candy. I hope she knows it wasn't a bribe. It was the only thing I could do that didn't feel like manipulation.

Jordan's text from last night still sits unanswered on my phone: *You see a therapist yet, or you still auditioning for guilt's greatest hits?*

Typical. I'd almost laughed. Almost.

I open my laptop and stare at my calendar. There's a board call at ten, a portfolio review at noon, and a hole where her name used to sit beside mine on every reminder. I drag the cursor over the space and type: **Dr. Levine 11 a.m.**

Then I hit save before I can change my mind.

The office smells like coffee and something citrus with a heavy dose of sanitizer. The waiting room is all soft lighting and low hums of quiet jazz, the kind of place designed to make you forget you're here because you broke something you can't fix. A young woman at the desk hands me a clipboard. I fill in the blanks: *Occupation, Emergency Contact, What brings you here today?*

I pause on the last one and finally write, *I don't know how to stop hurting people I love.*

When Dr. Levine calls my name, I expect judgment. What I get is a man in his sixties wearing a navy sweater and an expression that says he's seen worse.

We sit. He doesn't take notes right away.

"You're used to being in control," he says after a minute.

"Yes."

"And that worked, until it didn't."

I almost smile. "Something like that."

"What changed?"

"Someone," I admit. "She told me she was pregnant. I didn't believe her."

He waits. The silence stretches until it turns into confession.

"I accused her of lying. She left. She was right to."

Dr. Levine nods once, slowly. "What did you feel in that moment?"

"Fear." I rub a hand over my jaw. "And shame. But mostly anger at the idea that I'd been fooled."

"Did she fool you?"

"No."

"Then who did?"

It lands like a punch I didn't see coming. I swallow. "Me."

He lets the quiet hold a little longer. Then, "And what would you like to do about that?"

I stare at the floor. "Stop turning love into collateral damage."

He scribbles something this time. "Good goal," he says. "It'll take work."

"I know."

"Start here. Next time, bring me a short list of what you want to unlearn. Not everything. Just a start."

I nod. "I can do that."

Before I leave, he says, "Guilt can be a trip. Just don't mistake it for a home."

The wind cuts sharper when I step outside. The city feels louder, like it's been waiting for me to pay attention again. I walk to the corner café, which I haven't visited since before Christmas. The barista looks startled but smiles. "Long time no see, Mr. Monroe."

"Trying to change that," I say, and mean it.

I ordered peppermint tea instead of espresso. She blinks, then writes *Happy New Year* on the cup in green marker. There's a flyer on the bulletin board by the register some local nonprofit raising funds for new mothers. Usually, I'd walk past. This time I take one. I will give it to accounting to see about a donation.

I get in my car and head back to the office. Jordan texts me. *Did you go?*

At a red light, I text back. *Appointment kept.*

He replies with three dots, *then proud of you. Now go do something human before noon.*

Back at the office, Maxine intercepts me outside the elevator. "Levine?" she asks, deadpan.

"Yes."

"Good. Keep showing up. The company doesn't need another executive with a martyr complex."

"Noted."

She tilts her head. "And, Monroe, she received the packet."

My throat tightens. "How do you know?"

"She called the number for the counseling line. Didn't ask for anything else. Just verified coverage."

I exhale slowly, fighting the instinct to ask more. "Thank you," I say. "For handling it right."

Maxine's expression softens by a millimeter. "That's the job," she says, then steps back into the elevator.

The doors close, leaving me alone with the kind of relief that doesn't feel like victory, just oxygen.

By late afternoon, I shut down my computer, resisting the urge to stay buried in work. Progress isn't measured in hours anymore; it's measured in balance.

On my way out, I pass the new receptionist struggling with a stack of boxes. Usually I'd step around the obstacle and keep moving. Today, I stop. "You'll herniate yourself doing that," I say, taking half the load before she can argue.

Her expression flickers from surprise to cautious gratitude. "They're holiday decorations," she explains. "Facilities forgot to pick them up."

I carry them to storage and set them down gently. The glitter explodes across my sleeve like punishment. She laughs, small but genuine. "Thank you, Mr. Monroe."

"Just Asher," I tell her. "Mr. Monroe's learning how to behave."

She looks confused, but I leave before I have to explain it.

When I get home, I set croissants on the counter beside a fresh notebook. The first page reads:

Things I Need to Unlearn:

Control isn't love.

Silence isn't safety.

Fear isn't truth.

Below it, I add a fourth:

Forgiveness isn't something you earn once. It's something you build by showing up again and again.

I tape the list to the fridge. It looks ridiculous next to the takeout menus and wine-stained magnet that says *Work Hard, Play Harder.* Maybe that's the point.

The apartment hums differently tonight. I notice the drip of the faucet I've ignored for months. The way the city lights reflect off the counter is like scattered coins. I pick up a cloth and wipe the ring my scotch glass left behind on New Year's Eve. A small thing. But it feels like cleansing the crime scene of who I used to be.

For the first time in weeks, I call my mother. The conversation is awkward, halting, full of pauses that mean more than words. She doesn't know the details just that I "messed up with someone good." She says, *"Then be good enough next time she looks at you."*

I hang up feeling like she's both forgiven and scolded me at once.

I make tea. I sit. I breathe.

It's not much. But I don't reach for the bottle. I don't check her social media. I don't draft an apology I'll regret.

I just let the quiet be what it is—proof I'm finally learning how to live in it.

When I crawl into bed that night, I stare at the ceiling in the dark. Somewhere across state lines, she's probably asleep under a quilt, her world smaller, safer, softer than mine. I close my eyes and picture her hand pressed over her stomach, the same way it used to rest on my chest when she thought I was asleep.

I whisper into the dark, not as a promise but as a prayer.

"I'll be better next time."

Then I let the night keep me honest.

Chapter
Twenty-Seven

Candy

The kettle whistles before I'm ready to move. Mama calls it motivation. I call it harassment. Either way, it gets me out of bed. She's already humming in the kitchen, pots clinking like punctuation marks to her song.

The HR envelope sits open on the counter, its contents half-slid back inside like they might bite if I look too closely. I pick up my phone instead. The number from the packet glows on the screen. Call.

"Employee Wellness Network," a calm voice answers. "This is Leah."

"I, uh, got a packet from work. They said this was for ... counseling." My pulse is ridiculous.

She doesn't rush to fill the silence. "Would you like help finding someone near you?"

"Please."

She takes some basic information from me and responds with, "You're in luck. There's a licensed therapist nearby—Dr. Patel. She offers both in-person and virtual sessions, Fridays at two or Tuesdays at one. Which do you prefer?"

"Friday," I say. "Afternoon. Virtual, please."

She ends the call with, "Take the day gently."

Not good. Gentle. It lands exactly where I needed it to.

When I lower the phone, Mama's leaning on the doorway. She doesn't speak, just slides a mug of cocoa across the table. "Sounded like something brave," she says.

"Something necessary," I answer.

She smiles, small and proud. "Brave and necessary are usually the same thing. One just comes with more shaking hands."

By midmorning, the snow has eased into flurries, the kind that hover rather than fall. The Winter Market is mostly packed up now—banners drooping, leftover garlands clinging to poles like stubborn guests who won't leave the party. Bernice's old truck is parked sideways in front of the community center, tailgate open, full of cardboard boxes marked *DONATION SORT.*

She spots me the moment I turn the corner. "Candy Hart!" she hollers, as if I've been gone a decade. "You still own arms? Good, grab a box before I throw my back out."

I grin, tugging my gloves tighter. "You say that like it's optional."

"It's not." She thrusts a clipboard at me. "Sort the craft baskets from the food ones. Lord help the person who packed spaghetti sauce with crocheted baby hats."

The gym smells like lemon oil and old wood. Half the string lights are still up, their glow soft and crooked. We work side by side for a while, the scrape of tape and rustle of paper our whole conversation. The rhythm settles me. It's the kind of busy that doesn't demand talking.

"Market did better than ever," Bernice says eventually. "We'll have funds for the foster kids' drive *and* the food pantry."

"That's good," I say, meaning it.

She scribbles something on her clipboard, then passes it over. "Check my math for me? Eyes ain't what they were."

A line near the bottom catches mine: **Corporate Match Approved – Monroe Strategic Capital.**

My breath stumbles.

It's him. It has to be.

I look away quickly, pretending to reread the totals. "Looks right," I murmur.

Bernice, oblivious, keeps talking. "Whoever they are, they even covered all the supply costs for next year's waffle booth. Bless 'em."

"Yeah," I manage. "Bless 'em."

The rest of the morning blurs. We stack boxes, label bins, chase a runaway roll of tape that insists on living its own life. Kids from the elementary school run in and out with armfuls of mittens and laughter that feels like cocoa and snow. Each sound knocks a little more dust off the quiet I've been hiding behind.

When the last box is loaded into Bernice's truck, she hands me a paper cup of cider. "You doing okay, sweetheart? Folks miss seeing you around."

"I'm getting there," I say honestly.

"Good." She bumps my shoulder. "Keep getting there."

The walk home feels longer, though maybe that's just the weight of new thoughts. The world is white and bright, snowbanks glittering, chimney smoke drifting lazily against a pale sky. I pass the bakery, the post office, and the park bench where Daddy taught me to tie my shoes. Every corner feels smaller than I remember, and somehow that's comforting. You can't get lost when home keeps shrinking itself to fit around you.

Daddy's in the mudroom when I push through the door, brushing snow and hay off his jacket. He looks like he's been waging war with a stubborn latch in the barn. "Bernice work you hard?" he asks.

"She always does."

He nods toward the kitchen. "Your mama's makin' soup. Go sit before she decides you look underfed."

The house smells like rosemary and warmth. I drop my gloves on the counter and lean against the doorframe, watching Mama slice bread with surgical precision. She glances up, already knowing. "Friday, right?" she asks.

"Friday."

She exhales, slow and happy. "Good girl."

I roll my eyes. "You can't call me that while I'm growing a human."

"Fine," she says. "Good woman." Then she grins. "Still my baby."

After lunch, the quiet stretches. The kind that's heavy but not painful. I wander into the living room, drawn by the baby-name books spread across the coffee table. I hadn't meant to open them, but my fingers do it anyway.

The first book is glossy and ridiculous, with a cherub on the cover and categories like *Names That Manifest Prosperity* and *Names That Pair Well With Labrador Retrievers.* I laugh out loud. The sound startles even me.

I flip to G. *Gabriel. Gavin. Gemma. Grace.*

Grace.

I whisper it under my breath like it's a secret. The syllable feels soft, deliberate like something you earn, not inherit.

Mama's voice drifts in from the kitchen. "Find any good ones?"

"Maybe." I retrace the word. "Grace."

"That was your great-grandmother's name," she calls back. "Fierce woman. Used to chase off salesmen with a broom."

I smile. "Sounds right."

I keep flipping, though my heart's already decided. Grace isn't just a name. It's a reminder that what broke me doesn't have to define me or the baby. That maybe the whole point isn't forgiveness; it's gentleness. The kind Leah mentioned on the phone.

Later, I curl up on the couch with my journal, ink smudging beneath my thumb as the clock ticks steadily on the wall.

January Fifth

Things I Did Today:

Made the call.

Carried boxes without crying.

Didn't flinch when I saw his name.

Things I'm Learning:

Healing doesn't mean pretending it didn't hurt.

Hope doesn't always announce itself. Sometimes it hums quietly in the background.

Peace feels a lot like ordinary.

I set the journal aside and pull the baby-name book back into my lap, fingers resting on that one word. *Grace.*

Maybe that's what all of this has been about.

Grace for him, grace for me, grace for the space between.

I rest a hand over the place where a future is growing. "Hi, little heartbeat," I whisper. "We're finding our way."

Outside, snow taps the window, soft and rhythmic, like a promise being kept. In the kitchen, Mama hums again, that same tune I've heard all my life but tonight, it sounds like something new.

I feel it all at once: the ache, the hope, the fragile thread of beginning.

And for the first time, I believe it's enough.

Chapter Twenty-Eight

Asher

The city looks different when you stop seeing it as a punishment and start seeing it as a possibility.

It's still loud, still restless, still trying to prove something, but there's something new in the air, or maybe just in me. This morning, I notice things I've ignored for years: sunlight bouncing off wet pavement, the curl of steam from a coffee cart like ghostly fingers offering morning crawlers and cappuccinos. The world feels freshly scrubbed after last night's rain, every sound sharper, every smell more insistent. I walk the ten blocks to Dr. Levine's office instead of driving. It feels simple, steady like breathing. There was a time I called it a waste of efficiency. Now the rhythm of my steps feels like a kind of penance I don't hate. My shoes splash through puddles, and I catch glimpses of my reflection in store windows: a man in a dark coat, hands deep in his pockets, face open to the wind. Not polished. Not perfect. Just moving forward.

Halfway there, my phone buzzes. Jordan.

"You up?" he says when I answer.

"Walking."

"You mean voluntarily? Hell really has frozen over."

"I've got an appointment."

"Levine?"

"Yeah."

"Good," he says, voice softening. "Just don't treat it like a strategy session."

"I'll try."

"Try harder. And maybe get some sleep for once."

The line clicks dead before I can answer, but I'm still smiling when I put the phone away.

For the first time in a long time, I'm not walking *to* something. I'm walking *for* something. Dr. Levine's office sits in a narrow brownstone near the park, all exposed brick and creaky stairs. The waiting room smells faintly of cedar, coffee, and hand sanitizer; a strange combination that somehow feels safe. The receptionist offers a polite nod; I return it.

Inside, Levine is sitting cross-legged in a navy sweater that looks older than some of my investments. The same jazz record as last time plays softly from the corner, a saxophone line looping slowly and melancholy.

"Morning, Asher."

"Morning."

He waits until I settle in before speaking. "How's your week been?"

"Intentional," I say. "Not good. Not bad. Just... deliberate."

"That's an upgrade from numb."

"Yeah."

He gestures toward the notebook in my hand. "Did you bring your list?"

I pass it over. He reads the title without comment:

Things I Need to Unlearn

- Control isn't love.

- Silence isn't safety.

- Fear isn't truth.

- Forgiveness isn't something you earn once it's something you build.

He looks up. "Which one feels the hardest today?"

"Silence," I admit. "It's... easy. Predictable. It looks like control from the outside. Inside, it's just cowardice with better posture."

He studies me for a beat. "Who taught you that silence kept you safe?"

"My father." I don't even hesitate this time. "He believed if you never said the wrong thing, no one could hold it against you."

"And what did it cost you?"

"Everything honest," I say quietly. "Candy saw that. She saw through the polish and called it what it was. I didn't know how to let her stay after that."

"She saw you, and you ran."

"I didn't run," I say automatically, then catch myself. "Okay. I sprinted."

Levine's smile is small but genuine. "You're starting to recognize patterns. That's good. But recognition without repair just builds smarter walls."

"So what do I do?"

"You learn to speak differently. You learn to use your voice for truth, not defense."

"Easier said than done."

"Then let's make it easier done." He leans forward slightly. "Homework. Start a journal. Write everything you want to say to her—apologies, explanations, the things you'd never say out loud. Don't send it. Don't edit it. Bring it next week, and we'll sort through what's yours to carry and what's hers to choose."

I almost laugh. "You really think a man who works in finance needs a diary?"

"I think a man who mistakes control for love needs a language that doesn't involve ultimatums," he says, unruffled.

I exhale, nodding. "All right. I'll try."

"Not for her," he adds. "For you. Because the only way you ever get to be honest with someone else is by surviving honesty with yourself."

He lets the silence hang after that not heavy, but real. I find I don't want to fill it.

Outside, the air bites colder than before. The wind sharpens the edges of everything the skyline, the sound of tires on wet asphalt, the smell of hot dogs from a cart near the corner.

A barista recognizes me when I stop for tea. "Mr. Monroe, back again?"

"Need a pick me up," I say, and she grins.

While she pours, I notice a flyer taped beside the window: donations for the city's maternity shelter. I take a photo and text Jordan:

"Set up a standing monthly match through the foundation—New Mothers Fund."

He replies with a thumbs-up emoji and then:

"Proud of you. That felt human."

I smirk. *"Trying,"* I text back again, and keep walking. By the time I reach my building, my hands are stiff with cold, but I feel strangely awake. The city looks different when you stop seeing it as a backdrop and start treating it like proof that you're still here. That night, I sit at the kitchen table with an old notebook and a pen that leaks a little at the tip. I flip past a few empty pages until one feels right.

At the top, I write:

Things I Want to Say.

For a long time, nothing comes. Then

You were right. I didn't listen.

I thought believing you meant losing control, and I didn't know how to survive that.

I'm sorry for confusing caution with care, fear with reason, and distance with safety.

You didn't need saving. You needed to be believed.

My handwriting starts neat, then dissolves into something unrecognizable halfway down the page. I cross out whole lines, circle others. When I pause, I realize I've written something that wasn't meant for her at all:

I hope the baby likes snow.

I don't even remember writing it. I stare at it for a long time before closing the notebook. The ink is smudged from where my hand rested too long, but the page feels alive. Honest.

I slide the notebook into the drawer beside my keys. I'll bring it to Levine next week. Let him help me find what's apology and what's hope.

I wash the dishes, leave the TV off, and let the quiet stretch until it doesn't feel like punishment. The faucet drips. The city hums. For years, I've filled silence with noise; now I just listen. That's when I see it the photo magnet on the fridge. A grainy shot from a college bar, arms slung around each other, beers in hand, both of us too young to know how fast we'd break things. Torin and I. The ghost I've been dodging for a decade. He was there that night. The one I stopped talking about. The one that changed everything. I dry my hands, take a breath, and pull out my phone. His number is still saved. I don't know why. Maybe some part of me always knew I'd need it again.

My thumbs hover, then start typing.

Hey, Torin. It's Asher Monroe. I owe you a conversation. Are you free this week?

The three dots appear, vanish, reappear. Then:

Took you long enough. Friday, 6. Same bar?

Friday works.

I stare at the screen for a long moment after sending it. The fear I expect doesn't come. Just the quiet sense that maybe this is what healing looks like walking back into the rooms you once burned down and seeing if you can stand the smoke.

I put down my phone, turn off the light, and let the city hum.

For the first time in months, I don't feel like I'm standing still.

Chapter Twenty-Nine

Candy

The morning smells like coffee and cold air. Mama cracks the kitchen window "for circulation," even though it's thirty-two degrees out, and the wind sneaks in like a nosy neighbor. The steam rising from her mug turns my stomach, not in a dramatic way more like a soft, constant nudge reminding me I'm not the only one living in this body anymore.

"You sure you don't want toast?" she asks, already halfway to the breadbox.

"I'm sure." Just saying the word *toast* makes my mouth do a slow, quiet revolt. "Maybe crackers."

"Crackers, I can do." She slides the sleeve across the table as if she's passing state secrets. "Salted or unsalted?"

"Whichever makes me less tragic."

She smiles at that, relieved to find a laugh. "Salted it is." She sets a small bowl beside the crackers. "Peppermint candy. Probably illegal medical advice, but it helped with you."

I try one, let it melt against the roof of my mouth, and breathe through the wave. The peppermint steadies the edges. The smells of the kitchen coffee, soap, faint cinnamon tilt toward manageable.

"I've got the doctor this morning," I say, and the sentence drops something weighty and real between us.

Mama nods, wiping her hands on a dish towel she's nearly worried bald. "I can drive you."

"I'll be okay," I say. "It's only fifteen minutes."

"Text me when you're done." She hesitates. "Candy?"

"Yeah?"

Her eyes go bright. "I'm proud of you."

It lands like a hand on my back, warm and steady, guiding me toward the door.

The medical building sits on the edge of town, all beige walls and hopeful art. The receptionist wears peppermint-red nail polish and a tiny gold snowflake necklace. "First visit with us?" she asks.

"First official one." I tuck a pink curl behind my ear and try not to look like someone who might bolt.

She smiles and hands me a clipboard that could double as an upper-body workout. Family history. Meds. Do I smoke? Drink? Exercise? I circle *no, no,* and *walk sometimes,* and pretend that anxiety counts as cardio.

A nurse with kind eyes calls my name. Blood pressure. Weight. The scale tries to deliver judgment, but it fails; my body has other priorities now. She leads me into an exam room with a poster of a fetus the size of a lime. It's strangely sweet and alien all at once.

Dr. Morales knocks lightly before entering. She's late thirties, hair twisted into a quick bun, a smile that lands like reassurance.

"Candy," she says, shaking my hand. "Welcome in. I've read your intake forms and your clinic record. How are you feeling today?"

"Tired. Nauseous. Hungry, but only for crackers if they're shaped like boring."

"That's a very normal menu at your stage," she says, tapping a few notes into her tablet. "By dates, you're around eleven weeks. We'll confirm with measurements at your first-trimester screening. Have you started a prenatal?"

"Gummy vitamin," I say. "I can't swallow the horse pills without... drama."

"We love gummies," she says. "Two a day. Lots of water. Small, frequent meals. Avoid the greatest hits unpasteurized cheeses, high-mercury fish, sushi that isn't cooked, and deli meats unless heated. Ginger or peppermint can help with nausea. Pepcid if heartburn joins the party."

"Who invited heartburn?"

"Everyone's on the guest list," she chirps. "Okay. Let's listen."

The gel is chilly, and my breath goes thin while she slides the Doppler. Static. My own heartbeat, loud and bossy. Then another sound, faster, insistent. Like a hummingbird against a drum.

"There," Dr. Morales says, a grin flickering. "Strong and steady."

I don't realize I'm crying until she hands me a tissue without comment. It's not an ugly cry. More like something in my chest loosens the knot it's been working on and lets the future slip through.

"It's real," I whisper.

"It always has been," she says softly. "You just have to listen for it through the noise."

She runs through the rest efficiently and kindly: estimated due date in late July, lab orders, a first-trimester screening, and a nuchal translucency ultrasound at twelve to thirteen weeks, and a reminder to keep moving but not to be a martyr about fatigue. "You'll feel little twinges sometimes," she adds, "round-ligament growing pains. Annoying but harmless. If anything scares you, call."

Her pen pauses above the paper. "Support system?"

"My parents," I say. "And a friend or two. It's... new."

"That's support," she says. "We will be too. You're not doing this alone."

When I leave, the receptionist slides a small appointment card across the counter. I slip it into my wallet like it's something holy.

The grocery store on the way home feels like a small test of bravery. I make it through produce without crying at the sight of clementines (a win) and detour down the cracker aisle like a pilgrim finding her shrine. A woman from the church recognizes me near the butter. "You back for a while, honey?"

"For a while," I say, and she pats my elbow like that's precisely the right amount of promise.

Outside, the sky is a flat, pale gray that could snow at any minute. My breath ghosts in front of me as I walk to the car. I realize I'm not shivering. I'm steady. It feels suspiciously like hope.

At home, Mama has soup simmering. "How'd it go?" she asks, already bracing to be strong if I need her to be.

"Eleven weeks," I say, dropping the appointment card on the counter. "First screening next week."

Mama's hand flies to her chest anyway, like the moment is still happening. "I still can't believe it," she says softly. "That sound."

"Like wings," I say, and it makes her eyes shine.

Daddy comes in through the mudroom, dusted with hay and clean cold air. "Somebody's got good news?" he asks, scanning our faces like a weather report.

"Eleven weeks," Mama repeats, and he nods like he built that number himself.

"Tightened the legs on that porch glider," he says, pretending he's talking about hardware and not about peace. "You nap. Soup later."

I do, because rest isn't a suggestion anymore. It's an order. My body drags me under like a tide.

When I wake, the house is quiet and gold with the kind of late-afternoon light that forgives everything. I check the time. Ten minutes until my therapy appointment.

I make peppermint tea, open my laptop, and click the link.

Dr. Mira Patel is precisely as I remember from the bio photo I pulled up after Leah mentioned her name: calm eyes, tidy bun, cardigan that looks like it has pockets full of patience.

"Hi, Candy," she says. "I'm glad we could meet today."

"Me too," I say. And it's true. I didn't know therapy could feel like relief until now.

We talk about the appointment with Dr. Morales, the heartbeat that still seems to echo under my ribs. Dr. Patel doesn't rush the story. She lets it be as big as it felt. Then, gently: "Tell me about the hard part."

"Asher," I say, and the name doesn't cut me open this time. It just sits there, true. "He didn't believe me."

"You told him you were pregnant, and he doubted you. What did you feel in your body when that happened?"

"Cold," I say, surprised at how fast the memory returns. "Like falling through ice."

"And then?"

"I left." I straighten the corner of a notepad, a nervous habit I've never managed to break. "He said things he can't take back. I don't know if he meant them. I know I heard them."

"What part of you are you protecting by staying away?"

"The part that learned to be small to keep the peace," I say. "She's tired."

Dr. Patel nods once. "Good. I'm glad she's tired. Let's give her a job that isn't shrinking." She leans forward just a little. "I'm going to offer you two tools today, and you can tell me which you want to start with."

"Okay."

"The first is a boundary script. You write it ahead of time and practice it until your body recognizes the words like muscle memory. It's for if he reaches out, and you don't want to improvise when you're flooded. Four sentences. No apologies you don't mean. Want to try now?"

I swallow. "Yes."

"Good. Start with *I* statements. *I'm focusing on my health and the baby. I'm not ready to talk about us. If that changes, I'll reach out. Please respect that.*" She smiles kindly. "How does that feel in your mouth?"

"It feels weirdly powerful for four sentences," I say, and the corners of her eyes crease.

"Perfect. The second tool is a writing exercise. Not an unsent letter to him that can come later if you want it. I want you to write two very short birth announcements for your journal. One where he's in your life, one where he isn't. Name the constants. Circle what stays the same."

I blink. "That sounds... awful."

"And useful," she says. "It will show you what's yours, no matter what happens with him. Then you can decide from strength, not fear."

My eyes sting unexpectedly. I nod. "Okay. I'll try."

"Lastly, a small somatic practice for when the nausea and anxiety team up." She demonstrates: feet flat, one hand on heart, one on belly, inhale for four, exhale for six. "Tell your nervous system you're not in the office anymore. You're home."

We schedule next Friday's session. When the screen goes black, I sit there a minute longer, hand over hand heart and belly breathing like she taught me. The room comes into focus around me, the peppermint steam drifting, the soft tick of the hall clock syncing with the rhythm inside me.

On the counter, I line up the things that mean *next*: prenatal gummies, a stack of lab orders, the first-trimester screening appointment card, and the HR packet I've folded and refolded until the crease is an answer. I add a sticky note with Dr. Patel's tools:

Boundary Script (4 lines).

Two Birth Announcements.

Breathe, then decide.

Mama passes by, reads without reading, and kisses the top of my head like a benediction. "Want me to pull the quilt from the cedar chest?" she asks. "The bluebells one. It's softer than it looks."

"Please," I say, suddenly and fiercely needing soft.

While she's upstairs, I pull my journal close.

January 14   Things I Want to Remember

The heartbeat sounded like a tiny bird that already trusts me.

Dr. Morales said "strong and steady," and I believed her.

Dr. Patel said boundaries are kindness.

I can be gentle and firm at the same time.

I flip to a blank page and write **Two Announcements** at the top. My hand shakes a little, but I keep going.

A. *We're thrilled to announce the arrival of Grace Monroe, born on a July afternoon while thunder rolled politely in the distance. She arrived with a strong yell and a stubborn chin. Her* *mother cried. Her grandfather pretended he did not. Her grand-mother sang Patsy Cline. Everyone shared the joy. Her father was there, quiet and sure, and when he held her, she stopped yelling, as if she knew.*

I underline the things that feel like they could be true no matter what: *July. Strong. Thunder. Grandparents. Shared the j oy.*

B. *We're thrilled to announce the arrival of Grace Hart, born on a July afternoon while thunder rolled politely in the distance. She arrived with a strong yell and a stubborn chin. Her mother cried. Her grandfather pretended he did not. Her grandmother sang Patsy Cline. Everyone shared the joy. We were held. We were e nough.*

I circle *We were enough* and stare at it until the water clears from my eyes.

The baby-name book is still open where I left it, that soft, simple word catching me: *Grace.* I draw a star beside it. I add a maybe under it: *Miles,* if life has other plans.

After dinner, I take the trash out and stand on the porch longer than necessary. Snow starts up again small flakes, not showy, the kind that looks like dust until you feel it on your face. The neighborhood is quiet, the way winter makes everything quiet: not empty, just contained. A light goes on across the street. Somewhere, a radio plays something tinny and sweet.

I press my hand to my stomach, still barely a curve. "Hey, little heartbeat," I whisper to the snow. "We're okay. We're learning. I'll keep you safe, and I'll keep me safe."

The porch light hums. The flakes find my hair, my lashes, the edge of the quilt. Behind me, the house smells like cocoa, clean laundry, and the faintest hint of peppermint. I step back inside and tape the appointment card to the fridge beside the HR packet and the photo magnet of me at five, gap-toothed and proud. The three together look like a plan.

Before bed, I write the boundary script on a notecard and tuck it into my planner. I don't know if I'll need it. I know if I do, I won't have to find my courage on the spot.

Upstairs, I slide under the bluebells quilt and let the day settle. The nausea eases, the fatigue hums, the room grows soft around the edges. I breathe the way Dr. Patel taught me: in for four, out for six, hand to heart, hand to belly. *You're home,* I tell my nervous system. *You're home.*

Somewhere far away, under a different sky, a man I loved might be learning the same lesson in a different language. That's not my job to manage. Mine is simple, impossible, and daily.

Be steady. Be kind. Choose peace when I can find it.

I fall asleep between the heartbeat I heard this morning and the one I'm learning to trust again.

And for the first time since everything broke, I don't feel like I'm waiting for the other shoe to drop. I feel like I'm lacing mine for the walk ahead.

Chapter Thirty

Asher

The bar hasn't changed in twenty years. Same scuffed tables, exact string of lights no one's replaced since the Bush administration, same chalkboard with "IPAs" spelled wrong. It used to make me crazy; now it feels like evidence that not everything has to evolve to survive.

I take the booth against the wall—our old booth—and put my notebook beside me like it deserves its own seat.

I'm early on purpose. The air smells like hops and fried food, and the sound system's playing some early-2000s song that would've been on a party mix the year everything fell apart. I order water just to keep my hands busy. When Torin walks in, the room notices. I notice for the first time he hasn't changed much—broader, maybe, lines carved deeper around his mouth, but his eyes are the same. Steady, unimpressed, honest in ways that used to make me itch.

He spots me, lifts his chin, and slides into the booth.

"Monroe."

"Torin."

We sit in the kind of quiet that knows its own weight.

"Same table," he says finally.

"Couldn't risk ruining a classic."

He snorts. "You and nostalgia didn't have money riding on that bet."

The server drops off his beer and leaves us to it. "You not drinking?" he asks, glancing at my glass.

"Water's fine."

"Good." It's not approval, exactly more like relief.

He leans back. "All right. Before we start digging through the past, let's be clear. I'm here because you asked. Not to re-fight old ghosts."

"I'm not here to fight," I say. "I'm just done pretending none of it mattered."

He studies me the way he used to study balance sheets. Then he nods once. "Okay. Start where you should've started a decade ago."

"I'm sorry," I say, simple as that. "For what I said. For what I didn't. For turning on the only person who tried to keep me from drowning."

He takes a sip, doesn't rush. "About Lila."

"Yeah. About Lila."

The name leaves a bad taste in my mouth.

Back then, we were twenty and bulletproof. He was easy where I was sharp; I mistook the difference for balance. Then came Lila pretty, magnetic, the kind of chaos that flatters a man who thinks he can fix it. Six months in, she said she was pregnant. I believed her before the words finished leaving her mouth. Torin told me to wait. To breathe. I didn't. He's the one who found the truth an unsent email on a campus computer about "keeping Asher in line until the internship lands." He brought it to me like a friend bringing proof the fire's spreading.

But Lila moved faster. She said the baby was his, that we'd been in competition the whole time. I believed her. Called him a liar. Accused him of betrayal.

He didn't defend himself. Just walked out. And when she disappeared a week later, crying about a pregnancy that never existed, I built my new religion around the only sermon that made sense: *Never be caught off guard again.* I wore that rule like armor and called it self-preservation.

"You remember it, right?" Torin asks, voice easy but eyes sharp.

"Yeah," I say. "I made control look like a religion."

He nods. "You got real good at that."

"I thought keeping people out gave me the upper hand. Turns out it just meant I was scared."

"Welcome to humanity," he says dryly, and for the first time tonight, we both laugh.

He tips his bottle toward me. "So why now? Why reach out?"

"Because everywhere she was, you were," I say. "The office, the auction, outside the clinic. I told myself a story that made sense of it said you were doing it again. Being the good guy while I was falling apart."

He raises a brow. "And?"

"And it wasn't true," I admit. "You were just... there. Doing what decent people do when someone's hurting."

"Yeah," he says quietly. "That's all it ever was."

We let that sit awhile. The clatter from the bar fills in what we don't say.

"Tell me about her," I say at last.

He looks up. "Which one?"

"Start wherever you want."

He chuckles. "All right. Lila, then."

He tells it like a man who finally gets to close the file: the crying, the manipulation, the way she'd brag about me when I wasn't around. "You thought you were saving her," he says. "I thought you were just trying to outrun your own loneliness."

"That tracks," I admit.

"And Candy?" he asks.

I blink. "What about her?"

"Same story, different cast. You saw honesty and called it risk. You saw strength and called it a threat."

He's not wrong.

"I ran into her outside that clinic," he says. "She looked pale, but said she'd be fine. I believed her. Later that night, after you..."

"Lost it," I finish.

"Yeah. She was in the lobby when I came down. Still upright, barely. Said she had a place to go. I made sure she got in a cab. That was it."

I stare at the table. "You didn't tell me."

"You weren't listening to anybody back then," he says, not unkindly. "And it wasn't my story to tell."

We let that settle.

"You want to know what I actually held against you?" he asks finally.

"Please."

"It wasn't that you didn't believe me. It was that you didn't believe in yourself enough to handle being wrong. Pride's cheap. Repair's expensive."

It hits clean, not cruel.

"I'm trying to learn how to use my voice again," I say. "Not just to win."

He nods at the notebook beside me. "That's why you brought that thing?"

"Therapist homework. Write what I want to say. Figure out what needs to be said. Don't send it until I know the difference."

He grins. "For what it's worth, that sounds like progress."

We drift into easier territory. He asks about the firm, Jordan, and therapy. I ask about his consulting work nonprofits now, financial cleanup for people trying to do good without knowing how numbers work.

"Less soul-crushing," he says. "Fewer sociopaths in suits."

"Depends on the nonprofit," I say, and he laughs.

When the food comes, we both ignore it. The beer's half gone, my water's warm.

"You still think less of me?" I ask.

"Sometimes," he says easily. "Then I remember we were idiots in our twenties. The trick is not to stay an idiot."

"I'm working on it."

"Good. Because if you want to be the man who doesn't need rescuing, you don't get there by pretending the rescue never happened."

That one stings, but in a way I can use.

"I asked HR to reinstate Candy's benefits," I tell him. "No pressure. No angle. Just a clean offer of support. She took the counseling line."

"Good," he says. "You gave something without demanding the receipt."

He studies me for a second, eyes distant.

"I saw her at that auction," he says quietly. "She looked terrified, trying not to show it. That friend of hers the one with the microphone practically shoved her up there."

"Serina," I say.

"Right. Serina. You were sitting there like you'd forgotten how to breathe. Everyone else saw a fundraiser. I saw a woman trying to do something brave, and a man too scared of his own history to let it be just that."

I rub a hand over my jaw. "You're not wrong."

"She didn't look polished or fearless," he says. "She looked human. And somehow, that made her stronger than both of us combined."

I exhale, low and steady. "I never deserved her."

"No one deserves grace," he says. "That's why it changes people."

The word settles between us, heavier than silence.

When the check comes, I reach for it. He lets me. Outside, the cold bites deep. Our breath fogs the air.

"Same time next week?" he asks.

"Yeah," I say. "But you're buying."

"Deal."

He pauses before heading off. "Asher when you write her that letter, let someone else read it first. Not because you'll lie. Because you'll try too hard to sound noble, and she doesn't need noble. She needs real."

I laugh, startled. "You'd get along with Levine."

"Levine would bill me," he says, turning toward the corner. "Don't blow it, Monroe."

"I'll try not to."

He waves once without looking back.

At home, the city hums low through the windows. I set the notebook on the table and open it to the first page I wrote after Levine told me to start. The lines are messy, half cross-outs, half confessions.

I add one more:

You are not my penance. You're a person. I will act like it, even when I'm afraid.

I close the cover. Not because I'm done, but because I've said enough for tonight. Outside, the river catches a handful of lights and lets the rest sink. Somewhere under another sky, she's probably asleep. I don't pray often, but I do tonight. Let me keep choosing the quiet work. The apartment ticks with heat. The silence doesn't punish it steadies.

For the first time in years, I recognize the feeling humming under my skin. It isn't guilt. It isn't relief.

It's readiness.

Chapter Thirty-One

Candy

The world looks half frozen, half patient.

February in Connecticut means snow that doesn't know when to quit. The yard is patchwork now—bare earth in places where the sun's finally doing its job, white crust clinging to the shaded edges. When the wind shifts, you can smell mud and maple together, a promise that spring isn't gone, just late.

Mama says it's the "ugly-pretty" season. The time when everything looks tired, but the tired things are the ones that end up blooming first.

I'm trying to believe her.

The mail truck rattles past just after lunch, tires crunching through slush. I don't rush to the door anymore. Bills, coupons, the occasional card from someone at church that's all it's been for weeks. But today, the sound of the mailbox lid closing lands differently. The air feels... held.

I wait until the truck's gone before I go out.

The envelope is plain, cream-colored, edges soft from travel. My name is written in the same precise hand that used to sign contracts and birthday cards for employees. Not the messy scrawl of panic this is careful, deliberate.

Candy Hart.

No return address, but I don't need one.

The inside of my chest tightens like a reflex I haven't trained out yet. I stand on the porch long enough for the cold to sting my knuckles before I go back inside.

Mama's on the couch, knitting something that looks like a scarf but might turn into a baby blanket if left unsupervised. She looks up, eyes soft. "Letter?"

I nod. "Yeah."

She studies my face for a long beat, then nods toward the stairs. "Kitchen table's yours."

I sit, the envelope between my hands like a live thing. My tea goes cold beside me. The clock ticks, steady and judgmental.

It takes me three tries to open it without tearing the paper. The letter inside is two pages, ink dark, deliberate. His handwriting is neater than I remember, like he practiced it until it behaved.

I don't read it all at once. I can't.

The first line undoes me:

You don't owe me your time. You don't owe me your forgiveness. But if I could tell you one truth, it's that I'm not who I was when I let fear speak for me.

I breathe around it.

I believed my own damage was protection. I made you pay for it. I'm sorry.

There's more about therapy, about the notebook, about learning the difference between penance and repair.

Penance, he writes, *was guilt dressed up like effort. Repair is quieter. It's doing the work even when no one's watching.*

He never says *I love you.* He never asks for another chance. It isn't a plea or a performance.

It's a confession with both hands open no demand attached.

By the last paragraph, my throat hurts in that raw, quiet way that has nothing to do with crying and everything to do with being seen.

You don't have to write back. Just know that I'm still learning how to listen.

The signature is small, understated.

Asher

No flourish. No closing line about hope or faith or grace. Just the name that still lands somewhere between ache and home.

I fold the pages once, twice, and set them beside my mug. For a long time, I just sit there, tracing the creases with my thumb.

The radiator hisses. Somewhere upstairs, Mama hums along with the radio. Outside, snowmelt drips from the eaves in a slow, steady rhythm. The whole world feels like it's thawing one inch at a time.

Part of me wants to hide the letter away, pretend it never came. The scary part. The part that's gotten good at boundaries and breathing through triggers.

But the other part the one that heard that heartbeat through static and decided she could do hard things she wants to answer. Not to fix, not to forgive, but to acknowledge.

Dr. Patel's words echo in my head: *You can be gentle and firm at the same time.*

So I clear the table. Find the same kind of paper Mama uses for holiday notes. Sit with a pen until my fingers stop shaking.

I don't write much. I don't edit. I don't apologize for needing time.

Asher,

I got your letter. Thank you for writing.

I'm still working through things. Therapy helps. So does the sound of tiny bird heartbeats and peppermint tea. I'm learning that healing doesn't have to be loud to count.

I don't know what the future looks like, but I'm glad you're finding your path. Keep doing the work. Keep choosing the quiet kind of good.

Candy

I read it once and let it be.

No rephrasing. No second-guessing. I fold it, slip it into an envelope, and address it to Monroe Strategic Capital, because the only address I have for him is still the office. I almost laugh at that at how full circle it feels, this small piece of humanity routed through the very building where everything fell apart.

Mama comes in just as I'm sealing it. She looks at the envelope, then at me. "You sure?"

"Not about much," I say. "But this, yeah."

She nods, kisses the top of my head. "Proud of you, baby."

Outside, the sun's sinking low, turning the slush on the road to melted gold. I walk the few blocks to the post office, my boots leaving half-prints in the softening snow. When the letter slides into the dark, the sound is small but final, like a door closing gently instead of slamming.

On the way home, I stop at the park. The swings are still half buried in snow, but one creaks lazily in the wind. Kids' laughter echoes from somewhere down the street. Life, persistent as ever.

I rest a hand on the curve of my stomach. "He wrote, little heartbeat," I whisper. "We wrote back."

A breeze cuts through, cool and clean.

The world isn't fixed, but it's moving. So am I.

That night, I curl under the bluebell quilt. The letter sits on my nightstand, edges soft from my hands. I think about how forgiveness isn't a door you open it's a window you crack just enough to let light back in.

When sleep comes, it's dreamless and steady. The kind that means maybe, finally, the past is loosening its grip.

Chapter Thirty-Two

Asher

The city moves differently when the ice starts to give. Cars hiss through slush instead of crunching over it, and people walk faster, trading scarves for open collars. I match their pace, coffee in one hand, phone in the other, pretending I'm not waiting for a message I already know will come.

I used to fill mornings with work so I couldn't hear myself think. Lately, I walk. Ten blocks turns into twelve, and somewhere between the deli and the florist with buckets of tulips out too early, my shoulders climb down from around my ears.

My phone buzzes.

Candy: Morning. Morale check: how's your pen doing?

I smile before I can stop it.

Me: Functional. Writes honest sentences on command. Levine is impressed.

Candy: Look at you, getting gold stars. I have a question for you, but you're allowed to say no.

I stop at the corner even though the light is green. Therapy has a lot of rules, but one has stuck better than the others: breathe before answering. I do.

Me: Ask.

Candy: Anatomy scan next week. Dr. Morales says it's OK to bring one person. If you want to come, I'm OK with that. If not, we're OK too.

My chest tightens in a way that isn't panic. It's something cleaner.

Me: Thank you for asking me. I'd like to be there. Tell me what time and what you need from me. I can drive up or take the train. I'll wait in the lobby if that's easier.

There's a pause long enough for a February gust to cut through my coat.

Candy: Tuesday, 2 p.m. If you take the 11:06, you'll get here with time to spare. No gifts. No surprises. Just... show up. And peppermint tea if they run late.

Me: Done. I'll text when I'm nearby.

Candy: OK. Have a good day, Asher.

Me: You too, Candy.

I pocket the phone and keep walking. The city looks like itself again, messy and alive. Somewhere, a jackhammer starts. Pigeons argue over a bagel. I'm surprised by how steady I feel.

Levine raises one eyebrow when I tell him at the end of our session.

"She invited you," he says. "What does the invitation ask of you, specifically?"

"Show up on time. No surprises. Bring peppermint tea if there's a delay."

"And what does it not ask of you?"

"To fix anything. To make it perfect. To narrate the moment into something larger than it is."

He nods. "Good. Write before you go. Ten sentences you want to say, none of which you'll say out loud at the appointment. Then, after, ten sentences about what you heard instead of what you hoped to hear."

I make a face. "You like numbers."

"I like containers," he says. "They keep floods from becoming disasters."

"Thorin says the same thing, just with more sarcasm."

He smiles. "You have good mirrors right now. Use them."

Back at the penthouse, I put the notebook on the counter and write without the need to be elegant.

I want to say: I'm sorry again. I'm grateful to be invited. I will follow your lead. I don't deserve this, but I will try to be worthy of it. I hope the baby is healthy. I hope you're sleeping. I hope you're not carrying this alone. I'm learning to listen. I'm here because you asked. Thank you.

When I finish, the page looks like me. Not the past-tense version. The current one. That feels like the point.

Tuesday is bright and cold. The sidewalks in Midtown wear a thin glaze that looks slippery and behaves itself. I pack the peppermint tea bag in my coat like a talisman and take the 11:06. The train hums the way trains do when people have places to be and don't need you to know what they are.

Near Stamford, a toddler eats an apple slice with the focus of a CEO. Across the aisle, a college student writes flashcards with tiny, urgent handwriting. I write too. Not a letter, not a speech. Just facts.

Train arrival 12:28. Walk to clinic 12 minutes. Text Candy when within two blocks. Do not buy flowers. Don't bring anything she didn't ask for. Ask if she wants you in the room. Accept the answer. Be quiet. Follow. Breathe.

It's almost comical how much of my life used to run on improvisation and volume. Turns out, quiet is trickier. It asks for muscles I didn't use.

I text her when I'm two blocks out.

Me: Here. No rush. I'm early. Waiting outside.

Candy: Inside is fine. Less wind. Third floor. I'm a few minutes away.

The lobby smells like hand sanitizer and lemon oil. A kid kicks his heels against a chair and counts ceiling tiles. I sit two seats down from his mother, looking at nothing in particular. My heart is drumming slowly; I suspect everyone can hear, but no one looks up.

Then she's there, cheeks pink from the cold, scarf looped once around her neck, hair tucked into a beanie that tries and fails to tame it. The sight hits me like a memory I didn't know I was still carrying: the exact shape of her smile when she decides she's going to be brave.

"Hi," she says.

"Hi," I say, and it lands like a handshake, with us both setting the terms first.

We ride the elevator in a silence that isn't awkward. On the third floor, she checks in. I stand a little behind, not because I'm hiding but because I want the receptionist to see her first and me as an accessory she elected to wear.

"Do you want me in the room?" I ask, quiet enough that we could pretend I didn't if she needs to.

"I do," she says. "If you can be still."

"I can," I say, and I mean it.

A nurse calls her name. We follow. The exam room is warmer than the hallway, and the walls are hung with abstract art that looks cheerful on purpose. Candy perches on the edge of the table. I take the chair by the wall where she can see me without turning.

Dr. Morales knocks once and enters. She moves like someone who knows people rehearse disasters in their heads and is careful not to trigger them.

"Good afternoon," she says. "You must be Asher."

"I am. Thank you for letting me be here."

She nods. "We like supportive people. Today is the detailed anatomy scan. Long look at everything—heart, brain, spine. We measure, we listen, we celebrate. If the baby cooperates, we can talk about sex. If the baby doesn't, we try again later."

She talks Candy through the gel and the transducer as if she's narrating a cooking show. The screen comes alive in grainy grayscale. I've seen ultrasounds on other people's fridges, smeared in magnets and grocery lists. None of those prepared me for this.

There's a head. A spine like a string of pearls. A hand that floats up and seems to wave or punch or both. The heart flickers and makes a sound like someone drumming tiny fingers on a table.

I don't realize I've gripped my knees until I force my hands to relax.

"Looks good," Dr. Morales says. "Strong and steady. Measurements are right on schedule."

Candy laughs, a little breathless. I look at her instead of the screen for a moment because I want to remember this part too: the way her eyes go wide when she decides to let joy in.

They move through the checklist. The room is all soft clicks and numbers. Dr. Morales tilts the probe, squints, and grins.

"Baby is cooperative today." She glances at Candy. "Do you want to know?"

Candy breathes out. "Yes."

"Girl," Dr. Morales says. "Hello, little one."

The room shrinks and expands simultaneously. Candy presses her lips together like she's holding back something that will turn into everything if she lets it. I sit very still because still is the only correct answer.

"A girl," she says, like she's trying on the letters.

"Congratulations," I say. It comes out steady, thank god.

Dr. Morales prints a few images and hands Candy a tissue that is more thoughtful than effective. She towels off the gel, reviews the numbers, and makes notes that sound like reassurance turned into data. When she's finished, she looks at both of us.

"Healthy. Low-risk. Keep doing what you're doing. If the nausea lingers, try peppermint or ginger. Short walks. Lots of water. Call if anything feels off."

We thank her. In the hallway, the silence has a different weight. Not heavy. Full.

I hold the door for Candy without making a show of it. She slips the ultrasound pictures into a folder, as if she's protecting them.

"Do you have time," she asks, "for ten minutes and a peppermint tea?"

"I have time," I say.

We find a small café on the corner that sells hot drinks and heart-shaped cookies because the calendar insists on it. Candy orders peppermint. I order the same because it feels like the proper ritual. We take a table by the window. Outside, the sidewalk is a mosaic of ice and puddles. Inside, a little girl in a pink hat drops her mitten and makes an entire table of strangers coo.

"Thank you for coming," Candy says after a sip.

"Thank you for asking," I say. "I'll follow your lead on what happens with the pictures and how we talk about today. You tell me what's comfortable."

She studies me like a person reading instructions before assembling something that matters. "I'll text you a photo later," she says. "I might tell my parents tonight. I'm not ready for wider circles."

"Understood," I say. "Understood for as long as you need."

She nods, satisfied. "Dr. Morales was happy with everything."

"I heard," I say, and I can't keep the smile out of my voice. "Strong and steady."

She watches the steam rise from her cup, then looks up. "I wrote your word down in my journal last week. Repair."

I wait.

"I'm not promising anything," she says. "But I see you trying. Trying is not nothing."

"I'll keep doing it," I say. "Even if we end up only ever being people who share a kid and not a table."

Something changes behind her eyes that isn't pity or victory. Maybe it's respect. Perhaps it's relief.

"I picked a name," she says after a beat. "I'm not asking you to agree. I'm telling you where my heart has been. Grace."

The word lands like it's been here the whole time, waiting for a mouth to give it shape.

"It's beautiful," I say, because it is, and because I'm not sup-posed to tell her I had written it once in my notebook as a thing I hoped but had no right to ask for.

"Middle name is negotiable," she adds, a smile tugging at the corner of her mouth.

"I'll earn the right to be part of that conversation," I say. "No rush."

She nods, then laughs, small and startled. "Do you remember telling HR not to notify you if I called?"

"I do," I say, bracing, then relaxing when I see her expression is amused, not wary.

"Maxine told me after the fact," she says. "It was very... you. Efficient, stern, oddly kind."

"Maxine is the oddly kind," I say. "I'm the stern part learning to be less stern."

"You're doing OK," she says. "Don't get cocky."

"Noted."

We finish the tea and the ten minutes, then go to twenty. We don't talk about the day in my office or the lobby. We talk about train schedules, the weirdness of craving tacos at two in the morning, whether pink gets to be a color in Grace's closet, or if we will both rebel on her behalf and choose green.

When we stand, I don't reach for a hug. I don't ask for a timeline. I say, "Thank you for today," and mean it so hard it might leave a mark.

"Text when you get back," she says. "Not for me. For the part of me that is going to pretend not to worry."

"I will."

Outside, the cold snaps back like a rubber band. I walk her back toward the clinic because her car is in that direction. At the crosswalk, she stops.

"You look less... haunted," she says.

"Sleep helps," I say. "And writing instead of chasing perfection."

"Keep doing both."

"I will."

We stand there a second longer, two people who have learned to leave rooms without slamming doors. She lifts a hand in a small wave and heads across. I watch until she reaches her car and gets in. Only then do I turn toward the station.

On the train, I take the notebook out again, ten sentences about what I heard instead of what I hoped to hear.

I heard: healthy. I heard: a girl. I heard: Thank you for showing up. I heard: repair is noticed. I heard: no promises. I heard: boundaries. I heard: humor. I heard: a name that is more than a name. I heard: keep going. I heard: we can both be gentle and firm.

I close the notebook and look out the window. Connecticut slides by, all winter fields and the kind of light that makes everything look honest. My phone buzzes.

Candy: Tell Levine I graded your field trip. You passed.

I huff out a laugh that makes the college student across the aisle glance up.

Me: I'll frame the report card.

Candy sends a photo a minute later. It's the ultrasound, crisp and perfect. A profile. A hand. A caption with two words.

Hi, Grace.

I don't know if it's for me, for her parents, or for the future, but I read it like a prayer anyway. I put the phone face down and let the feeling be what it is. Not triumph. Not a promise.

Readiness.

In the apartment, I print the ultrasound photo Candy texted and tape it to the inside flap of the notebook. Not on the fridge.

Not yet. The notebook is private and honest. I close the book, put the kettle on, and stand at the window while the city does what it always does: moves. For once, I don't need it to move for me. I can move inside it, quietly, on purpose.

When the tea is done, I text Candy.

Me: Home. Thank you again. If you need anything that isn't a grand gesture, I can be helpful with groceries and coat drives.

She replies with a single check mark and a tiny heart, like a teacher stamping the corner of a quiz.

It's enough.

I put the tea on the table and let the steam lick the cool air. Somewhere in Connecticut, snow is melting into ankle-deep puddles that make kids shriek and parents sigh. Somewhere, a woman I hurt is choosing peace a little at a time. Somewhere, a girl named for a thing none of us can earn is practicing being a person whose heartbeat already sounds like a drum leading us forward.

I turn off the lights and let the city keep me company. Tomorrow I will wake up, write ten honest sentences, and send none of them.

Tonight I will be grateful that showing up can sometimes be enough.

Chapter Thirty-Three

Candy

I'm in the middle of arguing with a package of tissue paper when Mama announces, "We are not having a baby shower with naked tables, Candice Elaine. That is where I draw the line."

The tissue wins for the moment. It crumples instead of folding into the Pinterest-worthy puff I'm aiming for. "I did not realize your moral code began and ended at centerpieces."

"It begins with properly fed guests and cute decorations," she says, rummaging through a plastic tote like it insulted her personally. "Bernice says we can use the church fellowship hall for free, but she wants to know if you picked a theme."

"I'm growing a baby," I mutter. "Is that not enough?"

Mama gives me the look. The one that means she loves me dearly and will still whoop my ass for my smart mouth. "We could do little bluebird nests. Or those tiny book-themed showers. Or waffles. Bernice still thinks the waffle thing is adorable."

"Absolutely not," I say. "No more waffles. The universe has done enough with that pun."

She laughs, triumphant that I've joined the planning, whether I meant to or not. "Fine. What about 'Little Grace on the Way'? Bluebells and birds. Soft colors."

My hand stills over the tissue paper. We haven't told anyone outside the family the name yet. Hearing it out loud makes something flutter behind my ribs.

"It doesn't have to be Grace," she adds quickly, reading my face. "We can do neutral. 'Little Blessing' or 'Tiny Miracle' or 'Please Let This Kid Sleep Through the Night.'"

"No," I say softly. "Grace is good."

Her smile turns quiet. "Then Grace it is."

My phone buzzes on the table. I wipe tissue dust off my fingers before I pick it up.

Asher: Just got your lab results summary from the portal. How are you feeling about the iron thing?

I look at the half-finished tissue puff, then at the prenatal vitamin bottle on the counter, at the note Dr. Morales scribbled yesterday: Mild anemia. Iron supplement. More rest.

Me: Like someone who could nap on a laundry basket, it's fine. She did not look panicked. Therefore, I'm trying not to be.

Three dots appear, vanish, return.

Asher: I asked Dr. Morales if it was common. She said yes, very. Still, if there's anything practical I can do from here, let me know.

From here. He means the apartment he told me about at the last scan, the one ten minutes from the clinic, above a bakery that smells like fresh bread and ancient sugar. I stared at the picture of the narrow living room for a long time. Not flashy. Not some penthouse imported from New York. Just a clean rented space with a secondhand couch and a crooked view of Main Street.

I'm going to be in town more, he'd written. If that feels like too much, say so. I'll adjust. This is about showing up, not hovering.

Now Mama is eyeing me over the top of a bundle of yellow ribbon. "Is that him?"

"Yes."

"Is he behaving?"

"So far." I thumb another reply.

Me: You already did one practical thing. You didn't freak out in the office when she said monitor. That helped.

He'd stayed so calm yesterday, sitting in the chair by the ultrasound machine with his hands laced loosely, like he understood that panic would take up too much space in the room. Yesterday's scan still feels like it's happening in the corner of my vision. The exam room felt smaller than the last time. It could be the bigger machine. Maybe it was my nerves. The gel was cold. The lights were dim. Asher sat close but not too close, his knee a warm point of awareness near mine.

Dr. Morales rolled her stool into place. "Twenty-four weeks," she said with a smile. "Halfway, give or take. Ready to meet this kid in high definition?"

I nodded, though ready was a generous word. The screen came to life in shades of gray. At first, it was just shapes: static, shadows, outer space with better lighting. Then Dr. Morales pressed, angled, and the image sharpened into a profile. A nose. A curve of skull. A tiny fist stretching like someone waking from a nap.

I forgot how to breathe.

"There," she said. "Spine looks good. Heartbeat is strong. Four chambers." She pointed, narrating. "That's stomach. Kidneys. Femur. Everything is measuring right on track." Asher didn't speak. He just made a sound so quiet it could have been the air conditioning. She continued the scan, gentle and efficient. At the end, her expression shifted just a little. Not alarm. Focus.

"Okay," she said. "So, everything looks excellent overall. Strong heart. Good growth. One thing I want to keep an eye on—the placenta is a little low-lying right now. It may move up as your uterus grows, which is very common. I'm going to schedule another scan at twenty-eight weeks to make sure."

My stomach flipped. "What does... low-lying mean for her?"

"For now, nothing," she said calmly. "You might have a bit more spotting or pressure. We just don't want the placenta blocking the cervix later on. That's why we check again. If it doesn't move, we'll talk delivery options closer to the due date. But truly, this is a watch-and-see note, not a panic note."

Asher's voice stayed even. "Is there anything Candy should change in the meantime? Work, activity, travel?"

"Nothing drastic," Dr. Morales said. "Listen to your body. No heroics. If you have heavy bleeding, call us immediately. But I'm not grounding you from life, okay?"

I nodded. My hands were cold. Asher noticed; he slid a box of tissues closer, not making a big deal of it.

"Do you have support?" Dr. Morales asked gently.

"Yes," I said. "My parents. A therapist. Him." I jerked my chin toward Asher.

She nodded, satisfied. "Good. Then you're doing exactly what you need to be doing."

Afterward, in the parking lot, the winter air felt too thin and too sharp all at once. The snowbanks were receding into gray piles. Puddles had formed in the dips in the pavement, reflecting the sky.

"I'm fine," I said automatically.

"I know you are," Asher said. "And it's also okay if you're... not."

I watched a truck drive by, tires hissing through slush. "I knew there would be things to keep an eye on. I didn't think I'd hate the word monitor so much."

"Yeah," he said quietly. "Me too."

We stood there for a moment, not touching, watching our breath rise. Then he cleared his throat.

"I wanted to tell you something in person," he said. "But only if you have bandwidth to hear it."

"Bandwidth," I echoed. "Look at you with the therapy words. Go on."

"I've taken an apartment here," he said. "Month to month. Nothing dramatic. I can work remotely most of the time now. I told Jordan and Elliot I needed to restructure my schedule. They were... surprisingly supportive."

I processed that. "You moved here."

"I'm renting here," he corrected gently. "My life is still in New York. But hers," he nodded toward my stomach, "is here. I don't want to be a tourist in her story. I also don't want to hover over yours. So I'm starting with being nearby. You set the terms."

A dozen protective instincts flared at once. Then I remembered my own boundary script. I'm focusing on my health and the baby. I'm not ready to talk about us. If that changes, I'll reach out. Please respect that.

"I'm not ready for... anything else," I said. "No cohabiting, no moving in, no surprise nursery builds."

"I'm not offering those," he said. "I'm offering rides when you're tired and someone to sit in waiting rooms when you don't want your mom hovering. I'm offering grocery runs if your iron levels and the mid-afternoon crash gang up on you. If you say no, I'll adjust. Not argue."

He'd learned how to say things without asking me to make him feel better about saying them. It was disorienting in the best way.

"We can start small," I said finally. "No dropping by unannounced. Mama will tackle you with a broom if you show up without warning."

He almost smiled. "Noted."

I looked at him then, really looked. He was still Asher. Same jaw, same careful posture. But something in him had loosened, the way snow loosens when it finally gets tired of pretending it will last forever.

"Okay," I said. "We'll try it your way. Quiet. Respectful."

"Our way," he corrected. "Or not at all."

Back at the kitchen table, I blink away the echo of the ultrasound screen and type another reply.

Me: Practical thing you can do: stop reading medical journals about low-lying placentas. If Dr. Morales isn't panicking, you don't get to.

Three dots.

Asher: Guilty. I closed the browser. For the record.

Me: Good. Because my mother already tries to Google my symptoms. We can't have you both doing it. I'll end up not allowed to leave my bed.

"Does he know about the shower?" Mama asks casually, as if she didn't just stage-dive into my brain.

"No," I say. Then, "Not yet."

"Well." She loops ribbon through a punched hole in cardstock. "He might should."

"Might should is not a phrase," I mutter, because deflection is a hobby.

"It is in this house," she says. "Listen, baby. If he's going to be in that child's life, there's no harm in him meeting the people who already love her. It's not a proposal. It's potato salad and badly wrapped onesies."

The idea makes my stomach flutter in a way different from the baby's. Part nerves, part... something else.

"He'll be awkward," I say.

"Everyone's awkward at showers," she answers. "That's why we give them a punch and a job. He can keep track of who gave what for thank-you cards. He looks like he likes lists."

I snort. "You have no idea."

She pats my cheek. "Then ask him. If you want. Not for him. For you. So you don't look back and wish you'd let him stand in the corner and experience the horror of melted-chocolate-in-diaper games."

"We are not doing those," I say.

"We'll see," she says, which is terrifying.

I look back at my phone. My thumb hovers over the keyboard.

Me: Random question.

Asher: Those are the most dangerous kind.

That earns a small smile out of me.

Me: Mama and Bernice are planning a baby shower. Church hall, too much punch, probably at least five varieties of deviled eggs. It's in a few weeks. You don't have to come. But if you'd like to, you're invited.

There's a longer pause this time. I can almost see him at his little kitchen table, reading and rereading, careful not to type the wrong thing.

Asher: Thank you for inviting me. I'd like to come on one condition.

My shoulders tense.

Me: ...What condition?

Asher: You don't manage my comfort. If I feel out of place, that's my work. Not yours. Your only job that day is to let people celebrate you and Grace.

My throat tightens. He keeps doing that gently removing the invisible tasks I keep assigning myself.

Me: Deal. But Mama may assign you name-tag duty. Consider yourself warned.

Asher: I've faced hostile boards and activist investors. I can handle name tags.

I can see him trying to keep it light, not make the moment heavier than it already is. It works. Sort of.

Mama leans over my shoulder, unabashed. "Well?" she asks.

"He's coming," I say.

Her eyes get suspiciously shiny. "Good," she says briskly. "Then we'll need more chairs."

Daddy appears in the doorway like he scented the words baby shower from the next room. His jacket smells like cold air and hay when he shrugs it off and hooks it on the chair.

"What fool thing are we talking about now?" he asks.

"We are not talking foolish things," Mama says. "We are planning your granddaughter's shower. Asher's coming."

Daddy's jaw works for a second, the way it does when he's working out a response that won't get him in trouble.

"Good," he says finally. "A man ought to show up for the hard parts and the fun ones."

My heart stutters. "You're okay with that?"

"I'm okay with you deciding," he says. "And I'm okay with having a word with him if he forgets how to behave." He nods once, like he's already rehearsing a speech in the garage while he sharpens tools.

"Daddy," I groan, but part of me is relieved.

Later that afternoon, I lie on the couch under the bluebells quilt and let the low sugar headache pass. The house is warm. The snow outside is slowly giving up, sinking into patches of brown grass. From the kitchen, I hear the low murmur of my parents' voices, the clink of mugs, the stability of a life that has learned how to bend without breaking.

My phone buzzes again.

Asher: Meta-question. I never want you to feel like I'm hovering. Is that... actually helpful, or am I overthinking this?

I picture the narrow staircase, the bakery downstairs, the view of Main Street with its lopsided lampposts and stubborn Christmas lights someone forgot to take down.

He moved here quietly, not like a man making a grand romantic gesture, but like someone adding a line item to a budget labeled showing up.

Me: I like knowing you're close. I also like knowing you need at least thirty seconds' warning if I ever ask you for help, so you can put on your shoes.

Asher: Compromise achieved.

Another bubble arrives.

Asher: For the record, I'm proud of you. For the appointment yesterday. For calling Dr. Morales when the word monitor rattled you. For inviting me into your world in pieces instead of all at once. I know that costs you something.

I stare at that for a long time. The old me would have tried to wave it off. The new-contract Candy, the one Dr. Patel helps me practice being, lets it land.

Me: For the record, I'm proud of you too. For changing your life, not just your tone. For renting a regular person's apartment instead of flying in on a helicopter. For asking instead of assuming.

Three dots. Then:

Asher: You deserved a man who learned that sooner.

I exhale slowly.

Me: Maybe. But we both get the man you're learning to be now. Grace most of all.

When I put the phone down, the room feels different. Not bigger. Just... more possible. I rest my hand on my stomach. There's a faint thrum there now, not quite kicks, more like the brush of wings against the inside of a cage that's opening in slow motion.

"Hey, little bird," I whisper. "We're making room. Carefully. Slowly. On purpose."

Outside, a chunk of snow slides off the eaves and hits the ground with a soft thud. Meltwater trickles into the gutter in a thin, steady stream.

The world is still half frozen and half patient.

For the first time, it's allowed to be both.

Chapter Thirty-Four

Asher

The parking lot of the Pine Hollow Church Fellowship Hall is full. Too full. Cars, trucks, and a tractor for some reason. A sea of casserole dishes is being delivered through the double doors like offerings.

I am ten minutes early. Which, I'm learning, is the same as being late in Goshen.

I open the door expecting decoration. Maybe balloons. Maybe a banner.

What I get is... a pastel explosion.

There are tablecloths in three shades of pink. Deviled eggs in formation. A diaper cake taller than my dignity. A punch bowl that looks like it has its own gravitational field. Streamers. Ribbons. A sign that says **WELCOME, BABY GRACE** with enough glitter that it will haunt me until I die.

And Candy ...

Candy is standing near the punch bowl wearing a sash that reads "MOM-TO-BE" in cursive gold.

And a tiara.

A tiara.

She sees me. Her eyes widen; not flirty, not emotional, not wary.

Just: *Don't say a damn thing.*

Before I can even blink, she lifts a hand, index finger up like a warning.

"Don't," she mouths.

I raise both palms in surrender. Good choice, Monroe. Survival instinct.

Candy's mother materializes at my elbow like she was summoned by hormonal radar.

"Mr. Asher," she says brightly, gripping my arm like she's checking for structural integrity. "You made it!"

"Yes, ma'am," I say, because it feels required by law.

She beams, cheeks pink with pride. "Candy, honey, look who's here!"

Candy groans. "I told you he was coming."

"You didn't tell me he was coming *on time,*" her mother corrects, which apparently matters more than oxygen.

"Hi," Candy says to me, cheeks definitely warmed more from embarrassment than pregnancy glow. She gestures at the sash with a deadpan expression. "I'm being decorated against my will."

"It suits you," I say before I can stop myself.

She narrows her eyes. "I said don't."

"Noted."

Before I can dig myself deeper, a voice slices through the room like she owns it.

"Oh *fantastic.* They let the CEO in."

Serina.

Wearing sunglasses indoors. Holding a gift bag the size of a small dog. Strolling through a church hall like it's the Met Gala.

She marches straight up to me.

"Well, well, well," Serina says, adjusting her sunglasses but not removing them. "Look at you. Participating. Voluntarily. In public. With people."

Candy pinches the bridge of her nose. "Please don't bully him in front of the church grannies."

"Oh no," Serina says sweetly, "I'm going to bully him everywhere. Consistency is key in friendship."

She leans closer to me. "Smile, Monroe. You're terrifying the Baptists."

I exhale through my nose to hide the laugh. It fails.

Serina points at the name tags on the table. "Oh dear god. They have stickers. Don't let him alphabetize them."

"I wasn't."

"Lies," she says.

I peel off a sticker and begin writing my name, and before I can finish the A in ASHER, Candy's mother appears again, like she teleports.

"Wonderful handwriting!" she declares, snatching the sheet before I'm done and pressing it onto my sweater. "Now help me carry chairs."

Serina taps my arm. "Have fun, buddy."

Buddy.

I'm not sure whether that's encouragement or a threat.

The gift table is already buckling. Someone brought a stroller large enough to transport livestock. Mama—who will never accept any other title—gives me a job instantly.

"You have tall-man arms," she says, loading diapers and tissue-filled bags into my hands. "Stack these."

I stack.

"Not like that," she says. "Try again."

I try again.

"Mm-hmm," she says. "Better."

Candy watches from across the room, hiding a smile behind a cup of sherbet punch. Her tiara is crooked. Her sash is sparkly. Her hand keeps sliding to rest over her belly like she's holding the baby steady from the outside.

She looks tired. And more beautiful than I deserve to acknowledge out loud.

I'm tucking envelopes into a neat-ish pile when Serina reappears, sipping punch like it's top-shelf liquor.

"Monroe," she says ominously, "if you alphabetize the presents, I'm telling everyone here you cried at the ultrasound."

I freeze.

Candy hears and laughs until I worry she is going to shake Grace right out before it's time. The sound shoots through me like sunlight, bright and sparkling.

"I didn't cry," I mutter.

She raises an eyebrow. "Who would you believe?"

I choose not to respond. Smart.

I meet Candy's father midway through setting out the chairs.

He's tall. Weathered. Looks like he could bench press small vehicles. The kind of man who says ten words a day and means every single one.

He approaches slowly, like he's giving me a chance to run.

I don't.

He looks me up and down. Not impressed. Not hostile. Assessing.

"You're the father."

"Yes, sir."

He nods once. "Good."

That's it.

He walks off.

I exhale, possibly for the first time in four minutes.

Serina wanders over, whispering, "You survived. That man looks like he irons his jeans. Be grateful."

Candy snorts into her punch so hard she coughs.

Someone announces games.

I tense.

Candy tenses harder.

"Oh hell," she whispers.

Serina raises her hand like she's at an auction. "I volunteer Monroe for everything!"

"Serina," Candy hisses.

"What? He's tall. Let the man measure ribbon lengths with his wingspan or whatever wholesome nonsense you have planned."

I end up guessing the number of diapers in a jar, timing bottle-chugging races, and being used as a reference for "how long is

Asher's reach compared to the clothesline of baby socks" (long, for the record).

Candy sits in a folding chair of honor, looking mortified and delighted all at once.

When her mother fits the "MOM-TO-BE" sash more snugly around her belly, Candy locks eyes with me and mouths:

"I hate everything."

I mouth back:

"You look incredible."

Her cheeks go pink. She looks away.

Near the end, after the gifts and the cake and Serina loudly critiquing the punch ratio, Candy moves to sit beside me for a breath.

Her hand rests absently on her stomach again. Her lashes flutter like she's fighting sleep.

"You good?" I ask quietly.

"I'm full," she sighs. "And the baby is doing gymnastics. And Mama is trying to send leftovers home with people who live two hours away. So... yes."

I look at her tiara. "It's crooked."

She groans. "If you touch it, Asher Monroe, I will throw this punch at you."

I lift my hands. "Just an observation."

Her lips twitch.

She studies me for a long second. "Thanks for coming."

"Wouldn't have missed it."

"Even with Serina here?"

"That part I expected."

As if summoned, Serina swoops by. "I heard that. The two of you talking about me? Good."

Then she pats Candy's shoulder, squeezes my arm, and commands, "Don't screw this up, Monroe."

Candy freezes.

I swallow.

Serina walks away like she didn't just drop a live grenade in our laps.

Candy forces a breath, slow and steady.

"You okay?" I murmur.

"Yeah," she says. Then softer, "She's not wrong."

I don't push. I don't grab for meaning. I just sit with her in the noise and the warmth.

One slow inch at a time, she lets her shoulder lean into mine.

Just for a second.

But it's enough.

Chapter Thirty-Five

Candy

The house feels wrong the moment Mama and Daddy pull out of the driveway. Not empty but maybe a bit unbalanced. Like someone leaned on one side of my life and now everything tilts.

They left in a hurry but not panicking; Mama clutching her overnight bag, Daddy double-checking the gas and the directions even though he knows the route by heart. Two hours ago we received a call that Grandma wandered out of her assisted-living facility this morning and ended up two blocks away, confused, cold, and convinced she was late for school. The facility found her fast, thank god, but the director wants an emergency meeting with Mom and Dad as well as new assessments. There will need to be new paperwork filled out and a new care plan established.

Mama kept it together until she got to the porch and then had that trembly inhale that means she's trying not to cry. I hugged her, hugged Daddy, promised I'd be fine, promised I'd stay calm, promised everything would be okay.

I believed it at the time.

But as the taillights disappear down the street, something inside me slides off its axis.

The house creaks. The kitchen clock ticks too loudly. Somewhere in the house, the radiator clanks like footsteps. Typically it's nothing, but today, every noise feels loud and rough.

I've been alone plenty of times. I've spent years living on my own, but this is different, this isn't alone-alone. This is alone-and-pregnant, alone with the word *monitor* still echoing in my head from the last appointment. Alone with my parents out of state and too many thoughts and not enough oxygen.

"You're okay," I whisper to myself, standing in the doorway to the kitchen like the house might run away if I blink. The air feels thick. My heart does this fluttering skip that Dr. Patel says is anxiety, not doom. Still, my nerves don't appreciate the nuance. I try to shake it off, know I am being silly. I should go upstairs, maybe nap, maybe fold laundry. It has been piling up in my room lately.

I make it halfway up the stairs before my knees go soft and my head starts to swim.

Nope. Not normal. Not okay.

I sit down heavily on the step fast enough the thud echoes.

My hands won't stop trembling.

My breath feels tight at the top, like it can't drop all the way down.

My vision does this weird halo thing.

Grace flips, a slight startled movement that sends another bolt of panic through me.

This is fine. It's fine. It's fine.

It's not fine.

I grip my phone so hard I can feel the case edge digging into my palm. My first instinct is Mama. I scroll to her contact. Stop. Delete the half-typed message. They're already halfway to Rhode Island. They'd turn around. They'd panic. I'm not doing that to them.

Serina.

She's at work in New York and definitely incapable of calm.

My thumb hovers.

No.

I scroll again.

A name sits in the middle of the screen, steady as a heartbeat.

Asher.

My stomach swoops.

I shouldn't bother him. I shouldn't make this his problem. I shouldn't...Grace shifts again, and a wave of dizziness sweeps over me so fast I almost gag.

I hit CALL before I can think it through.

The phone rings once.

"Candy?" His voice is alert, sharp, not panicked but close. "What's wrong?"

I try to speak, but everything comes out thin. " I-I don't know. I can't... breathe right. Everything's spinning."

He's already moving. I can hear it in the echo behind his voice, like he's grabbing something, keys maybe, coat, shoes.

"I'm coming. Stay on the phone."

"No, you don't you don't have to."

"I'm already running."

There's wind on his end of the line. Footsteps. A car horn. He is *actually running through town* for me.

I squeeze my eyes shut. "Asher..."

"Candy, listen to me." He's breathless but steady. "I'm three blocks away. Sit down if you're not already."

"I'm sitting," I manage. "Halfway up the stairs."

"Good. Keep breathing. In through your nose. Slow. You're not alone. I'm almost there."

Something hot pricks the back of my eyes. Not fear this time. Relief.

Bone-deep, devastating relief.

"I'm at your street," he pants. "Two houses down. Keep talking."

"I'm okay," I lie.

"You're not," he says gently, "but you will be."

The front door slams open.

Boots on hardwood.

Then he's taking the stairs two at a time until he drops to his knees right in front of me.

He's flushed, chest heaving, hair messed like he ran face-first through a wind tunnel. But his eyes, those stay steady.

"Hey," he says softly. "I'm here."

I try to laugh, but it breaks into pieces. "You... you ran."

"You called." He shrugs like it's obvious. "Of course I ran."

The trembling starts again. I press both hands to my stomach. "I don't know what happened. I'm dizzy. My heart won't slow down. Mama left, and then everything felt wrong. And I know it's stupid but—"

"Stop," he says gently. "Nothing about this is stupid."

I swallow hard. "I didn't want to bother you."

He looks at me like that might be the saddest thing he's ever heard. "Candy... you are not a bother."

My breath catches.

He keeps his distance, not touching, letting me lead. "Can I sit next to you?"

I nod, grateful that he's here. He sits, close enough for warmth but not taking up space. I feel the heat of him like a hand on my back.

"Okay," he murmurs. "We're going to breathe together. Ready?"

I copy his inhale.

Slow.

Deeper than mine.

Then exhale.

The edges of the room come back into focus.

"Good," he says. "Again."

We do it three more times before my hands stop shaking.

When the worst of the storm settles, I tuck a strand of hair behind my ear. "Grandma wandered today."

His brow softens. "Oh, Candy."

"The facility called. Mama and Daddy had to go. I told them I'd be fine, and then five minutes later, I wasn't."

"That would rattle anyone," he says. "You're not made of stone."

I bite my lip. "I hate feeling like this."

"I know," he says. "But it doesn't mean anything is wrong with you. It means you're human, pregnant, and scared."

That lands harder than it should.

He watches me quietly for a moment. Then his voice drops lower. "Candy... you can't stay here alone."

Every instinct tries to argue. "I don't want to be a burden."

"You're not." His tone is soft but unshakable. "Come stay with me."

I blink. "Asher.."

"Listen," he says, leaning forward just enough to meet my eyes. "Not forever, but you and Grace should not be alone tonight. Or tomorrow. Or until you feel steady again."

My throat tightens.

He doesn't push further. He doesn't reach for my hand. He just waits, letting me breathe in the quiet between us.

I whisper, "Okay."

His shoulders drop, like he's been holding his breath since I called. "Okay," he echoes. "Let's get your things."

He stands first, offering a hand; not grabbing, just offering. I take it. He pulls me up gently, keeping a palm on my elbow until I'm steady.

I stop in the doorway of my room, suddenly embarrassed by the mess of half-folded laundry.

He shakes his head. "Candy. You're allowed to live in your house."

We pack together.

He folds my bluebell quilt like it's priceless.

He grabs my vitamins, my chargers, and my oversized hoodie that should probably be retired.

Ten minutes later, he carries my bag downstairs, one hand on my elbow again to guide me. When we reach the bottom, he pauses at the door as realization dawns.

"I ran here," he says quietly. "My car's a few blocks away. I'm going to go get it and bring it to the front door. Sit on the couch. Stay warm. And stay on the phone with me the whole time."

I nod, too wrung out to argue. He helps me back to the couch, tucks a throw blanket around my legs, and presses my phone into my hand like it's an oxygen mask.

"Call me," he says. "Right now."

I do. His name lights up my screen the second he steps outside.

"I can hear you breathing," I say.

"That's the point," he answers, a little breathless already. "Talk to me so I know you're okay. Tell me what you see."

"The lamp," I say, staring at the soft yellow glow. "My shoes are by the radiator. The snow is starting again."

"Good," he murmurs. His footsteps crunch faster. "Keep going."

I tell him anything that isn't fear. The blanket. The silence. The way Grace shifts low in my abdomen like she's listening to.

"I'm at the car," he says after a minute. Breath puffing. Door thunking open. "Stay with me another thirty seconds."

The engine starts. Five minutes later, headlights wash across the front window. My chest loosens in a way I don't admit out loud.

A moment later, his car rolls up to the front door, idling like a promise. He jogs inside cheeks flushed, hair damp from melted snow and holds out his hand to help me up, but he lets go as soon as I'm steady.

"Okay," he says softly. "Let's get you home."

Outside, the air is cold and smells like melting snow. He guides me toward his car, not touching unless I waver.

He opens the passenger door. "Seat warmers are on."

A laugh sputters out of me. "You really prepared for every scenario."

"No," he says. "Just the ones that matter."

When I'm buckled, he jogs around to the driver's side, slides in, and glances over.

"You ready?"

I nod. "Yeah."

He drives slow, careful over patches of slush, one eye on the road, the other flicking to me every few seconds like he's making sure I'm still breathing.

At his building, he parks close, helps me out, and walks me inside. The bakery downstairs smells like cinnamon and butter.

The stairwell is narrow and warm. His apartment is small but tidy, books stacked, kettle on the counter, blanket on the couch.

He locks the door gently behind us.

"Make yourself at home," he says. "I'll take the couch, you take the bed. I won't take no for an answer."

I hesitate. "Asher... thank you."

His expression is soft. "Anytime you need me, you call. You don't have to wait until you're shaking."

My chest goes tight again but this time it isn't panic.

This time it's... something quieter.

Something safe.

I set my bag down, slip off my shoes, and curl onto his couch. He hands me a glass of water and adjusts the blanket so it covers my feet.

He doesn't hover.

Doesn't fuss.

He just sits on the floor nearby, leaning against the couch, phone face down beside him, presence warm and steady like fireplace heat.

Grace kicks, gently, like she's reminding me she's here too.

I rest a hand on my stomach and whisper, "We're okay."

Then, softly, I add, "Because he ran."

Asher glances back at me, not hearing the words but sensing the shift. "You need anything?"

"No," I say. "Just you being here."

He nods, like that's the easiest thing he's ever been asked to do.

"Then I'm here."

I didn't realize how off-kilter I've been until now, when something finally settles.

Chapter Thirty-Six

Asher

Candy falls asleep on my couch before midnight under the blue quilt she brought from home. Her light pink hair falls across the pillow and a hand is tucked beneath her cheek, the other resting over her stomach in a protective arc I don't think she even realizes she makes.

I sit on the floor beside her, not hovering, not touching, just close enough she'll know she isn't alone if she wakes up scared again.

The apartment is dim except for the single lamp I left on. Downstairs, the bakery is silent for the night, resting until the early-morning crew arrives. The whole building feels still, like the world is holding its breath. Candy's breathing evens out slowly, settling from the shaky, uneven rhythm she had when she first walked through my door.

I watch her chest rise and fall. Slow. Steady. Safe.

Thank god.

Every time I replay her voice on the phone—thin, trembling, terrified—my pulse spikes all over again. I still feel the cold air burning my lungs from the sprint to her house. Still hear the echo of my boots on her stairs. Still see her trying so hard to be brave while her entire body shook. I'm not a panicker. I've built a life around not panicking.

But today? I came close.

Around one in the morning, I force myself to stand. My back cracks, reminding me I'm not twenty anymore. I grab a pillow from the closet, toss it on the floor next to the couch, and lie down.

I keep her in my peripheral vision for hours. Just in case. When I open my eyes again, there's a sliver of pale winter light sliding through the blinds and Candy sitting on my couch, awake and looking around my apartment like she's trying to decide if this is real. She sits up slowly, one hand pressing to her lower back. The blanket slips, and she adjusts it automatically, careful, gentle, the way she touches everything connected to the baby.

I clear my throat so I don't startle her. "Morning."

She turns, and the smile she gives me is soft. Small. Still a little tired around the edges. "Morning."

I push myself up, wincing when the floor makes an unwelcome argument against sleeping on it at my age. "Hungry?"

"Maybe."

"I can make breakfast."

Her eyebrows go up. "Can you?"

"I can try."

She laughs a sound I haven't heard in what feels like a month, even though it's been less than twelve hours. "Okay. Try."

I head to the kitchen. It's small, but I know every inch of it like a map burned into my palms. I pull eggs from the fridge, get the kettle heating, and put toast in.

Her eyes follow me around the kitchen, curious. It makes something in me tug, and I can't help but smile.

"I'm not a chef," I warn her. "So lower your expectations."

"I don't have expectations."

"Well, lower them anyway. I've learned quite a few things since being here, but I'm still far from competent." The eggs stick a little. Whatever. They are still tasty. I make her plate first, add fruit and water because she needs it, then set everything on the counter with a simple, "Sit."

She sits and tries some eggs. Her face softens. "These are actually good."

I try not to look as relieved as I feel. "Told you. Edible."

She eats slowly. I watch her without being obvious. Or I try, at least. When she sets her fork down and leans back, her hand drifts to her stomach again. That instinctive gesture. The one that tightens my throat every time.

"You slept?" I ask.

"Some."

"You woke up once."

Her eyes widen slightly. "You...noticed?"

"Candy." I rest my elbows on the counter. "You were shaking on the stairs yesterday. I wasn't going to sleep until I knew you were okay."

The silence that follows is thick but not uncomfortable.

"Thank you. I appreciate it," she says quietly.

"You don't have to thank me."

"I do."

Her voice is so soft I feel it more than hear it.

We clean up together. She washes. I dry. It feels startlingly domestic, like we've done this a hundred times even though we never have.

She hesitates over her laptop. "Mind if I work here today?"

"You live here right now," I say before I think. "You don't have to ask."

A faint pink touches her cheeks. She settles on the couch and starts typing. I take my laptop to the dining table and pretend to work, but every few minutes she shifts positions, one hand rubs her stomach or she sighs softly, and I look up like a reflex.

Around noon, she flinches slightly.

Not in pain more surprise.

I'm on my feet before the thought fully forms. "You okay?"

Candy bites her bottom lip. "Just... a kick."

I freeze. "Can I...?"

It comes out more careful than I intended. She nods, a quick, nervous motion.

I move slowly, sitting beside her but not crowding her. She puts her hand on her stomach. I wait until she reaches for my wrist and gently guides my palm over.

Warmth. Soft cotton. The faintest trembling in her fingers.

Then, a small thump.

Nothing in my entire life has prepared me for what that does to me.

My breath catches, sharp and stupid. Candy watches my face, and when she sees the realization settle, her expression warms, softens, steadies.

"She's strong," I whisper.

"She is."

I pull my hand back slowly, reluctantly. "Thank you."

She nods but looks away, as if it made her feel something she's not ready to admit.

Me too.

Definitely me too. After a quick call with Dr. Morales, she looks calmer. More grounded.

"She said it's normal," Candy reports. "And I shouldn't be alone until the dizziness stops."

Relief hits me so hard it borders on dizziness of my own. Not because she needs me. But a medical professional finally said out loud what I've been screaming in my head since yesterday.

"Good," I say. "Then stay here."

She hesitates, just a breath. "Okay."

It's a tiny word. But it feels important. We work for a few hours again. I answer emails. Approve budgets. Review numbers that suddenly feel stupidly irrelevant when compared to the sight of her curled into the corner of my couch, wearing my spare socks. When she starts drooping sideways, eyes half lidded, I stand.

"Bed," I say.

Her nose wrinkles. "I can sleep on the couch."

"No," I say gently. "You'll sleep better in the bed. I'll take the couch."

"You don't have to."

"Candy." I meet her eyes. "I snore."

She snorts. "Okay, that's fair."

I lead her to the bedroom. It's small, warm, tidy except for the stack of books on the nightstand. She sits on the edge, hands clasped loosely over her bump.

She looks so small. And so strong. And so breakable in a way that makes every protective instinct in me sharpen.

"If you need anything," I tell her, "I'm right outside."

"I know."

"Even if it feels stupid."

She shakes her head. "Nothing about yesterday was stupid."

I swallow. "Good, we agree. Now call me if you need anything."

I linger in the doorway a second too long. She gives me a tired smile, soft and careful.

"Goodnight, Asher."

I can't help the warmth in my chest at her quiet goodnight. "Goodnight, Candy."

I close the door gently and return to the couch. I leave a lamp on in the hallway so she won't wake to darkness.

I sit.

I listen.

I breathe.

For a long time, all I can think about is the way her voice broke when she said she didn't want to bother me. The way she said okay when I asked her to stay. The way her daughter—our daughter—kicked against my hand like she was saying she's here too.

And it hits me, slow and unstoppable:

I'm not scared of yesterday. I'm scared of how right it felt to run to her. How natural it feels to have her in my home. How quickly I've rearranged my life around the idea of her and Grace being safe. When the clock hits midnight, I stretch out on the couch, folding one arm under my head, turning so I keep the bedroom door in view.

Just in case.

Snow taps against the window probably the last of the season. The lamp glows warm and steady. And somewhere in the room behind that door, Candy is sleeping. Breathing. Safe. For the first time in hours, I close my eyes. And everything in me settles. Not because she's here, but because she called, she trusts me.

Because I ran and I'd run again.

Every single time.

Chapter Thirty-Seven

Candy

I wake up warm.

Warm in a way that feels not quite mine, like stepping into someone else's sweater or someone else's peace. The blanket is soft against my cheek; the air lightly sweet with something baked hours ago. The light filtering through the blinds is smooth and pale. The kind of morning light that doesn't ask anything of you yet.

I ease the bedroom door open and step into the quiet of the hall, then into the living room beyond.

Downstairs, the bakery hums like a heartbeat beneath our feet: mixers, footsteps, muted voices, the occasional clang of a tray being set down. Life is already moving. A rhythm steady enough that some small, hidden part of my body falls in step with it.

For a second, I forget where I am.

Then I see him.

Asher is asleep on the couch, back against the cushion, head tilted at an uncomfortable angle. His arms are crossed, but not in that defensive, CEO way. His stubble is darker than usual, shadowing his jaw. His hair is messy from sleep, soft curls falling forward like they've given up trying to be disciplined.

He looks... human. Really human. And tired. And gentle. Grace shifts a slow roll, like she's stretching in a warm cave she's taken over. My hand slips instinctively over my stomach, exhaling, long and steady.

The anxiety that drove me to the stairs, tight, sharp, overwhelming, feels like it's sitting several feet away now. Watching. Not pouncing. Like a creature that's lost its nerve.

I shift slightly, and the blanket rustles. Asher stirs immediately, blinking awake like someone who's trained himself to surface fast.

His eyes land on me.

He sits up straighter. "Candy. Are you okay?"

His voice is soft, but alert. Protector mode. It should annoy me. It doesn't. It feels natural.

"Yeah," I say. "Just... awake."

He scrubs a hand over his face, smoothing sleep from his features. He looks at me again, slower this time. "How do you feel?"

"Better," I admit. "Like my brain finally hit the reset button."

He nods slowly. Relief loosens his shoulders. "Good."

There's something in the way he looks at me—careful, relieved, steady—that makes my chest ache.

"You hungry?" he asks.

Before I can answer, something warm and sweet drifts up through the floorboards. Cinnamon. Brown sugar. Yeast. A smell like Christmas morning and fairytales and every good thing a bakery can do to a pregnant person's self-control.

My stomach reacts before my mouth does.

"I... think the bakery is trying to seduce me," I whisper.

Asher freezes. "What do you smell?"

"Cinnamon rolls," I say reverently. "Fresh ones. The gooey kind." My mouth is already watering. "I would commit crimes for one."

He blinks once processing, calculating, deciding and then stands so fast the blanket slips off his legs.

"Stay right here."

"Asher, you don't have to "

He's already grabbing his keys. "I know. I'm doing it anyway."

I laugh, helpless as he shoves on shoes and heads out the door with a determination I've only ever seen when he's confronting a boardroom full of billionaires.

Five minutes later, the door swings open again and warm air rushes in around him, carrying that holy smell with it.

He's holding a small bakery box like it contains state secrets.

"Mission accomplished," he says, a little breathless. "And I brought backup," he says, opening the box and turning it to face me.

Inside I see two cinnamon rolls so soft the icing is sliding off, a breakfast sandwich on homemade bread, and a cup of cut fruit. "For nutrients," he mutters defensively as he follows my gaze.

My whole body lights up.

"You're a saint," I tell him, already reaching.

He smirks, setting everything carefully on the coffee table. "Pretty sure saints don't bribe pregnant women with pastries, but I'll take it."

The first bite hits my bloodstream like a spiritual event. Someone could propose to me right now with a cinnamon roll, and I'd say yes before they finished kneeling.

Asher watches me with this small, quiet smile like he's relieved to see me enjoying anything, like the day before isn't breathing down my neck anymore.

"It's good?" he asks.

"Marry me," I mumble through a mouthful, and his laugh cracks the room open.

We eat together, me inhaling cinnamon sugar, him politely eating fruit like a responsible adult. My blanket drapes over my lap, and every few minutes he adjusts it without comment, like he can't help making me a little more comfortable.

It's the softest morning I've had in months.

Warm. Quiet. Careful.

Halfway through, Grace pushes against my ribs a sharp little jab.

"Oh," Asher says softly, watching my stomach like it's a miracle. "Is that...?"

"Yeah," I say, pressing a hand over the movement. "She's saying good morning."

Something in his expression melts, tender and almost reverent. It's unfair how good he looks when he lets himself feel things.

When we finish, I stand, planning to rinse my plate, but he intercepts me.

"You sit," he says. "I've got it."

I sit.

Because maybe just for a minute I need someone else to have it.

While he rinses plates, I glance around his apartment. It's small but warm. Plants on the windowsill that he absolutely didn't buy himself. A soft gray throw blanket. Books stacked in uneven piles. A notebook left open on the counter, pen resting on the page he must have been writing last night.

The normalcy of it settles around me like a second blanket.

After breakfast, I finally ask the question sitting in my mouth.

"Asher... is it really okay if I stay here? At least until Mama and Daddy get back?"

His answer is instant. "Yes."

I blink. "No hesitation?"

"None." Then, like he remembered he's a responsible adult, he clears his throat. "Unless you have concerns."

"No boundaries issues?" I ask, trying to hide the quake in my voice with a smile.

He lifts one eyebrow; the contract-lawyer one. "You set the boundaries, Candy. I follow them."

That shouldn't make my chest go warm. It does.

"Okay then." I pull in a breath. "Let's... outline terms."

He straightens like I've just handed him a multimillion-dollar merger. "I'm ready."

"Separate sleeping spaces."

"You get the bed," he says immediately. "Nonnegotiable. I'll take the couch."

"Fine." I fold my arms like I'm pretending this is formal. "Next clause: no hovering."

His mouth twitches. "Define hovering."

"Any variation of pacing, checking, peeking, monitoring, or staring at me like I might combust."

He considers this. "I reserve the right to emotionally hover from across the room."

"No physical hovering," I clarify.

"Agreed."

I nod. "Next. No touching unless I ask."

His expression shifts soft, reverent, like the words mean more than I probably understand yet. "Of course."

"And last..." I hesitate. "No checking on me every five minutes. No stealth wellness audits. No pretending the kitchen requires reorganizing so you can accidentally be in the same room."

One corner of his mouth lifts. "So what I hear is presence allowed; surveillance prohibited."

"Exactly."

"I can work within those constraints." He extends a hand between us, palm up. "Anything else to negotiate?"

I stare at his hand for a breath that feels longer than it is. I don't take it. I don't need to.

"I think that covers it," I say softly. "For now."

His shoulders ease like he's been holding tension since he found me on the stairs and finally gets to release it.

"Then we have an agreement," he murmurs.

And somehow, god help me, I believe him.

It feels dangerous to believe him, but I do.

A shower sounds good. Necessary, even. He gestures toward the bathroom like it's a sacred space he's proud to offer.

The hot water and citrus-scented soap loosen something knotted inside me. When I emerge wearing one of his oversized shirts the only thing that doesn't pinch or pull around my belly he freezes.

Not in lust.

Not in shock.

Something gentler. Softer.

"You look…" He trails off, searching for a word that won't make things weird. "Comfortable."

"I am," I say.

He exhales like that genuinely matters.

I curl onto his bed afterward, exhaustion pulling at me like a tide. The sheets smell like detergent and something cedar-leaning, and it makes my arms go loose and heavy.

"Can you stay?" I ask quietly. "Just while I fall asleep."

His whole body seems to soften. "Yeah," he murmurs. "I'll be right here."

He sits in the armchair in the corner, notebook in hand, pen quiet. His presence is steady enough to anchor the room. My eyes drift closed almost instantly.

Just before the darkness takes me, I whisper, "I feel safe."

I don't know if he hears it.

But I feel his breath catch.

And that's enough.

Chapter Thirty-Eight

Asher

Candy sleeps for almost three hours. She's been here long enough now that I don't sit sentinel the way I did the first night. I stretch my legs out in the armchair, book open but mostly forgotten, letting the apartment settle around us. Every so often, I glance over, just a glance, not the anxious checking from before. She's curled on her side, one hand resting over the round curve of her stomach. Grace shifts beneath her palm in a quiet ripple. She's wearing my shirt, which shouldn't undo me the way it does. The oversized cotton hangs loose over her hips, soft and pale against her skin. It was clean, tucked in the drawer with the backup shirts I keep for emergencies. Now it's hers. It looks like it belongs on her. Like she belongs in this room, this bed, this life. I inhale slowly. Don't get ahead of yourself, Monroe.

When she finally stirs, blinking awake in the dim afternoon light, she looks softer. Less guarded. Less weighed down by invisible things she refuses to let anyone carry. "Hi," she murmurs.

"Hey. How do you feel?" She stretches carefully, considering my question seriously.

"Better."

"Good," I say, and I mean it more than any word I've said this week.

She sits up, hair mussed, shirt slipping off one shoulder. I look away because I'm trying very hard to respect her boundaries, and I don't trust myself with the sight of her collarbone right now; the irony isn't lost on me. She pushes her hair back, twisting it up into a clip. "What time is it?"

"After one."

Her eyes widen. "Seriously? I haven't slept that long since before the third trimester turned my spine into spaghetti."

"You needed it." I stretch my legs a little. "Your body finally insisted." She glances at me in the armchair and frowns softly.

"Have you been sitting there this whole time?"

"Mostly." I shrug. "I didn't want you waking up in the apartment alone. I thought it would be slightly scary if I wasn't here."

Something warm flickers across her face. Not surprise, but definitely gratitude. I stand, giving her space. "You hungry?"

She nods immediately. "Starving. Like I could eat whatever is left in that bakery and still want more."

"Good," I say. "That's a healthy sign. I'm glad you're getting your appetite back."

She smirks. "Look at you. Mr. Prenatal Expert."

I cough. "I read things."

She stands carefully. I stay close but don't touch unless she wobbles. She's steadier today. Still tired, but stronger. I make grilled cheese and manage to only over toast one side. She slices apples and scoops out generous portions of peanut butter. We share lunch at the small kitchen table where I usually work. She props her feet on a chair. Grace kicks, and she presses a hand absently over the bump.

"You okay?" I ask.

"Just stretching. She's getting bossy in there."

I grin without thinking. "Good. A Monroe trait."

Her eyebrow lifts. "Excuse me?"

I freeze. "Not that she has to take my name," I blurt. "Or that she will. Or that she...."

She laughs softly. "Relax. No matter what name she ends up with, she's a Monroe, but she's also a Hart."

I exhale, relieved and mortified. When we finish eating, she stands too fast and wobbles. I catch her elbow instinctively.

"Sorry," she murmurs.

"You don't need to apologize for being human."

She chews her lip. "I don't like feeling fragile."

"You're not fragile," I say quietly. "You're pregnant. And anxious. Those are different things."

Her gaze flicks up. "You're very calm."

"I'm terrified," I say honestly. "But I'm calm on the outside because that's what you need."

She stares at me for a long moment, like she's seeing something she didn't expect. Before she can respond, her phone buzzes. "Mom?" she says, answering. I head toward the counter, pretending I'm not listening, but I am. "Yes," Candy says softly. "Okay... okay... no, I'm okay. I'm with Asher." Her mother must say something because Candy gives a soft huff of laughter. "Yes, he's behaving." A pause. Then, "I'll stay here until you get back. Promise." Her voice softens. "I love you too."

Her shoulders settle as she ends the call, looser and relieved, the kind of breath a person takes when the ground under them stops shaking. "She's okay," Candy murmurs. "Grandma's okay. They're keeping her overnight for more tests, but she's safe."

"Good," I say, and I feel it, honest and unfiltered relief for her. "That's really good."

She nods, fingers smoothing over the curve of her stomach. Grace answers with a tiny kick. Candy's expression softens, quiet and inward, like she's listening to something only she can hear. Then she looks around the apartment, not in that cautious, uncertain way she did before. Now it's like she's taking stock of a place she actually occupies. Her vitamins are lined up by the sink. Her folded blanket is draped over the back of the couch. Her overnight bag sits unzipped on the chair, half her things already blended with mine. She's settling in. Not asking. Not apologizing. Just existing here.

Something shifts in her expression, slight but unmistakable. A kind of easing. A type of choosing. She lifts her gaze to mine. "This feels less scary today," she says quietly. "Being here."

I nod once, slow and careful. "Good."

"I didn't realize how loud my brain has been," she adds, thumb brushing absently over the fabric of my shirt she's wearing. "And here it's just quieter." Her voice wavers on the last word, and she clears her throat like she's embarrassed by the honesty.

"You don't have to explain it," I say. "You're allowed to feel safe somewhere."

Her eyes flick to me, soft and a little startled, like she wasn't expecting understanding and doesn't quite know what to do with it. She sits back against the couch cushion, letting the tension drain from her shoulders. "I'm not used to this," she admits. "Not being alone with it."

"With what?" I ask gently.

She hesitates, fingers curling into the blanket. "Everything. The thoughts. The what-ifs. The panic that hits out of nowhere.

It feels stupid saying it out loud." "It isn't stupid," I tell her, and it comes out rougher than I intend. "It's human."

Her breath catches, just a little, and if that doesn't undo something in me, nothing will. She blinks down at her stomach again, Grace rolling beneath her hand. "I think she likes it here," she says softly. "She barely kicked yesterday, and now she's doing a whole dance routine."

"She likes cinnamon rolls," I say lightly. "She's my kind of girl." Candy laughs, and it's real, warm enough that my chest loosens in the way it only seems to around her.

She shifts on the couch, settling deeper into the cushions. "What now?" she asks, not in a lost way but in an open one. "Just exist here with you?" "If you want," I say.

"We can keep it simple." She exhales, long and slow.

"Simple sounds good." I nod toward the TV. "There's an entire contest dedicated to gingerbread structures collapsing under humidity."

Her lips curve. "Sold."

But she doesn't pick up the remote yet. She watches me instead, quiet and searching, like she's cataloging the ways this is different from anything she has known before. And when she finally leans into my side, it's subtle. Barely there. The lightest brush of her shoulder against mine, like she's testing the weight of comfort. I don't move. I don't breathe. I just let her settle.

Because this, this small trust, this shift toward me, feels like the real beginning.

Chapter Thirty-Nine

Candy

I wake before the sun.

Not from panic. Not from a bad dream. Not from a noise I've convinced myself means something awful.

Just... naturally.

For the first time in months, that feels like a miracle. The room is dim, warm, and familiar. Mama's bluebell quilt is wrapped around me, soft from a hundred washes. His apartment still carries that faint cinnamon scent that drifts up from downstairs every morning, mixed with something comfortable and clean that just feels like him.

When I stretch, slow and careful, Grace nudges back like she's saying good morning.

"Hi, little bird," I whisper, rubbing where she presses.

I slip out of bed and wander into the kitchen, blanket trailing behind me.

Asher is already there.

Of course he is.

He stands at the counter in plaid pajama pants, hair rumpled, holding a mug of coffee while he watches Main Street on the other side of his window. The morning news plays on mute behind him. It's the quiet version of him the one that exists only here, where no one needs anything from him except presence.

This version of him is increasingly dangerous to my emotions.

He turns when he hears my footsteps, and the smile he gives me is soft enough to melt bone.

"Morning," he says.

"Morning." I pull the blanket tighter. "Been up long?"

"Not really." His gaze sweeps over me once, assessing without hovering. "Did you sleep okay?"

"I slept," I say, grinning. "Like... real sleep."

He exhales, slow and relieved, and I realize he's been waiting for me to say that.

"Good," he murmurs.

I sit as he makes tea without asking peppermint, steeped exactly right. Two weeks of living here, and a rhythm has formed around us without either of us naming it. My parents texted once they were back home: *Stay where you feel supported.*

And somehow... I do feel that here.

Asher glances over his shoulder, pulling out a pan.

"Ready for breakfast? Toad in the hole?"

"Always hungry," I say, because pregnancy has made that my brand.

His mouth curves. "Tapeworm with opinions?"

"Exactly."

He starts cooking unhurried, focused. I watch him, warmed in a way I have no vocabulary for.

He sets the plates, sits across from me, and asks, "Feeling okay today?"

"Yeah," I say, surprised how true it feels. "I really am."

"Good. Let me know if that changes."

I sip my tea, gathering courage, and then, carefully, I say, "I was thinking..."

He raises a brow. "Dangerous."

I roll my eyes. "If I'm going to keep living here, and I want to, maybe Grace should have... a space."

Something shifts in his expression.

"A space," he repeats.

"Not a full nursery, just... something more than my suitcase and vitamins and an ultrasound picture stuck to your fridge with a donut magnet."

He turns fully toward me, leaning back against the counter.

"Candy," he says softly, "you can have more than a corner."

My breath catches.

"I don't want to take over your apartment," I whisper. "You already gave up so much space when I moved in and...."

"I didn't give up anything." His voice is calm and confident. "You're part of this place now. Both of you."

Right on cue, Grace kicks.

I swallow. "Okay. Then will you... help me pick out some things? Crib, changing table, whatever babies actually need, so I don't accidentally order something that requires a physics degree to assemble?"

His grin is instant and warm enough to undo me.

"I would love to," he says. "Just say when."

"Maybe today? If you're free?"

"Jordan's covering everything this morning," he says. "I'm yours."

Something deep inside me settles. Steady. Safe.

I go get dressed. He meets me at the door with my coat, helping me into it like it's second nature.

It kind of is now.

We step into the crisp morning air. Our hands brush. On instinct, I slide my fingers into his. He squeezes once. Not too tight. Not too much. Just enough.

"Remember," he says gently, "we don't have to get everything today. We can take our time. We'll figure it out together."

Together.

The word lands softly in my chest, threading itself through everything I haven't been ready to name.

We head toward the baby store. The store is bright, enormous, and immediately overwhelming.

Rows of cribs.

Strollers that look like luxury vehicles.

Baby monitors with features I swear NASA uses.

"Asher," I whisper, clutching his sleeve, "what is all this?"

"Several industries convincing new parents they'll fail without thousands of dollars of equipment," he says calmly. "We'll pick what actually matters."

My shoulders drop, tension easing. We start with cribs.

I'm drawn to a simple white one—clean lines, soft edges. He touches the rail, testing it gently, as if he's evaluating an architectural blueprint.

"This one," he says. "It feels safe."

My heart wobbles.

Next, rocking chairs.

I try one. It squeaks so loudly the associate across the aisle jumps.

Asher's expression flattens. "Absolutely not."

I dissolve into laughter and try another– plush, beige, perfect.

"Oh," I breathe. "This one."

His face softens. "Then we'll take it."

We pick out bedding with tiny bluebirds because Grace has been little bird in my head and heart.

Then we hit the stroller aisle, which is chaos.

He test-drives three of them down the sample lane with the focus of a man preparing for a triathlon.

"This one turns well," he says, taking a sharp corner that makes an older lady applaud.

I laugh until I have to sit down.

We scan everything into a cart–simple, practical. A crib. Chair. Sheets. A few soft clothes. A changing pad. Nothing excessive.

Not a whole nursery. Not a declaration. Just... space for her.

And maybe for me too.

At the register, I catch his sleeve gently.

"Asher?"

He pauses, turning toward me fully.

"Thank you," I say quietly. "For helping. For... this."

He studies me for a long moment warm, steady, unwavering in that way he only ever is with me.

When he speaks, his voice is low, sincere.

"Candy... taking care of you and Grace isn't an obligation. It's..." he searches for the right word, breath catching just slightly, "it's a privilege. You two are the most important people in my world. Helping you isn't something I *have* to do. It's something I'm grateful I *get* to do."

My heart stumbles. He doesn't reach for me. Doesn't push. Just offers the truth, soft and open.

"I just want you to know," he adds gently, "you never have to face any of this alone. Not anymore."

I swallow, the words settling deep.

His gaze flicks to my belly, softening in a way that makes something inside me tilt.

"I may have missed the first few months," he says quietly, almost like a confession, "but I don't plan on missing another moment. Not if you'll let me be here."

And god, I feel that everywhere. He loads the boxes into the car, steady and sure. When he closes the trunk, he turns to me with that soft, disarming smile. "Ready to go home?" he asks.

Home.

The word lands quietly. Deeply. Right where it belongs.

I nod. "Yeah. Let's go home."

Chapter Forty

Asher

Candy is laughing, the kind she makes when Grace kicks hard enough to surprise her. She is standing by the counter in my T-shirt, rocking back and forth like she is already soothing a newborn instead of a thirty-seven-weeks-and-some-change belly.

I'm halfway across the room, watching her the way I always do, like she is the center of gravity and I'm just trying not to fall over.

"Are you sure we shouldn't double-check the hospital bag?" I ask for the eleventh time.

Candy rolls her eyes. "Asher. We have three hospital bags. One just has snacks. You are nesting harder than I am."

"I just don't want..."

But I don't finish, because suddenly she gasps.

Not a little gasp.

A full-body, startled, oh-no gasp.

My heart slams into my throat.

"What? Candy, what is it? What is wrong?"

She looks down.

Then back up at me.

Her eyes are huge.

"Asher... my water just broke."

Everything in my body stops working.

Everything.

The world goes silent, except for some high-pitched ringing I'm not sure is external.

Then everything explodes into motion.

"Oh my god," I choke out. "Okay. Okay. We trained for this. We have a plan. Where is the plan?"

I spin in a circle. Why am I spinning? Spinning does not help. Nothing is where it should be. The apartment is suddenly a FEMA disaster site. "THE BAG. THE CAR. SHOES. WHY DO I NOT HAVE SHOES ON?"

"Asher." Candy tries not to laugh but absolutely laughs. "You need to breathe."

"I am breathing!"

I am not breathing.

"Breathe," she repeats, holding the counter.

"Oh my god, you're in pain. Are you in pain? You're pale. You're too pale. Sit down. Or stand up? Do you want to stand?"

Why am I asking her to stand? She's already standing.

"Asher," she says gently, "you need to get the keys."

Right. The keys.

The keys to the car.

Where are the keys?

I tear cushions off the couch. I open drawers. I check the fridge. WHY? WHY WOULD THE KEYS BE IN THE FRIDGE?

Candy snorts. She actually snorts.

"They are on the hook, sweetheart."

I whirl around.

There they are. On the hook. The same hook they have always been on.

I grab them, triumphant. "WE HAVE THE KEYS."

"Great," she says, smiling through another tightening breath. "Now maybe the bags?"

Right. The bags. I grab all three at once like an overburdened pack mule, slinging straps everywhere while Candy waddles toward the door.

Her face tightens. She grips the wall. My stomach drops straight through the floor and into the bakery.

"Contraction?" I whisper.

She nods. "Yeah. They're starting. I thought they said this was supposed to take a while with your first."

And something inside me shatters with fierce, overwhelming determination.

"Okay," I say, my voice steadier than I feel. "Okay, Candy. I've got you. I swear I've got you."

We make it down the stairs slowly, me hovering like the world's most frantic helicopter. When we reach the bottom, she stops again, pressing a hand to her belly.

I cup her back before she can sway.

"You're okay," I whisper. "You're okay. I'm right here."

She meets my eyes.

"Asher," she says softly.

"Yeah?"

She gives me a trembly smile. "Do not freak out."

I immediately freak out inside.

But I nod. "No freaking out. I'm solid. I'm a fortress."

"You're vibrating," she deadpans.

"I'm a vibrating fortress."

Another contraction hits. She leans into me, her forehead against my chest. And for a split second, just one, the world stops spinning.

It is just her.

Her breath.

Her strength.

My love.

The words hit me like a fist to the chest, but I don't have time to fall apart, because she sucks in a sharp breath.

And we are moving again.

By the time we reach the hospital curb, my hands are shaking so badly I can barely put the car in park.

Candy grips the door, breathing through another contraction, her forehead pressed to the window.

"It's okay," I whisper, even though nothing in me feels okay. "We're here, Candy. I've got you."

She nods once, jaw clenched. Brave. Always brave.

The second I jump out and round the car, an orderly is already jogging toward us with a wheelchair.

"Is this the mama?" he asks.

"YES," I bark. "THIS IS... THIS IS HER. HELP."

"Asher," Candy murmurs, embarrassed. "Please stop yelling."

"I'm not yelling," I say. I am absolutely yelling.

They get her into the chair. I grab the bags. All of them. Why do we have this many bags?

We roll through the automatic doors, and everything smells like disinfectant and fear and hope and things I cannot control.

The nurse looks calm. Candy looks brave.

I look like a terrified Victorian husband seeing childbirth for the first time.

They move us into a delivery suite, the lights too bright, the machines too loud.

A nurse helps Candy into a gown while I stand uselessly in the corner, trying to remember how to inhale without choking on it.

"Vitals look good so far," the nurse chirps.

"See?" Candy whispers. "We're okay."

But her hand grips mine too tightly, trying to borrow steadiness from a man who has none left.

When another contraction hits, she folds in on herself, her breath hitching.

"Okay," the nurse says, switching tones instantly. "That one was strong. Let's get the doctor."

They get her into bed. I stroke her hair, whispering anything that sounds like comfort.

"We're okay," I murmur. "You're okay. I'm right here."

"I know," she whispers, but she sounds small. "I'm scared, Ash."

I kiss her forehead. "I know. I've got you."

She squeezes her eyes shut, breath shaking.

I don't know when the doctor comes in. Everything starts blurring.

Her blood pressure monitor starts beeping. Too fast. Too loud.

The doctor frowns.

"Let's try repositioning," she says tightly. "Candy, sweetheart, I need you to lie on your side."

Candy tries.

Her face drains.

My heart drops straight through the floor.

"Is Grace okay?" she gasps. "Is she okay? Tell me she's okay."

"We're watching her," the doctor says. "Right now, I need to focus on you."

Right now.

Like this moment is the one that matters.

"Is something wrong?" I choke out. "You aren't saying anything."

The doctor gives me a look that is calm but not reassuring.

"Baby doesn't love how things are going," she says carefully. "And Mama's numbers are telling me we need to move quickly."

Move quickly.

Move now.

Candy's eyes fly to mine, wild and terrified.

"Asher..."

"I'm here," I say, squeezing her hand. "I'm right here. Candy, I'm not going anywhere."

A nurse touches my shoulder.

"Sir, you cannot come past this point. We'll update you as soon as we can."

"No," I breathe. "No. No, no, no."

Candy reaches for me as they start to push her toward the doors.

"Asher…"

"I've got you," I choke. "Candy, I've got you. Please… just…"

Her fingers slip from mine.

The doors swing closed.

And she's gone.

The room is too quiet after that.

Too bright.

I am standing, sitting, pacing, choking, praying. Minutes stretch like hours. Every second feels like something is unraveling inside me.

The doctor returns wearing the expression I've come to hate. Gentle. Measured. Too carefully arranged to be good news.

"Asher," she says quietly, "we delivered your daughter."

My heart stops. Everything in me goes still.

"She's doing well," the doctor continues quickly. "She's full term and breathing on her own. Ten fingers, ten toes, and more than a little upset at being evicted."

Breathing on her own. My knees almost give out.

"But," she adds carefully, "because of the complications during labor, we brought her to the NICU for observation. Her vitals dipped for a moment, and we want to keep a close eye on her to make sure she transitions perfectly."

Complications.

NICU.

Observation.

None of these words say danger, but none say safe either.

I swallow hard. "Can I... can I see her?"

"Yes," the doctor says gently. "We'll take you to her in just a moment."

Her tone shifts almost imperceptibly.

"And Candy?" I ask, my voice barely a whisper.

The doctor's smile falters for a fraction of a second, there and gone, but enough to tear something inside me.

"She is stable," she says, choosing each word with care. "But we aren't done working on her. The team is doing everything they can."

Stable. Working on her. Everything they can.

None of it says she is okay.

I nod numbly, because nodding is the only thing keeping me sane.

"Let me see my daughter," I manage.

"Of course."

A nurse appears beside me, ready to lead me down the hall.

And just like that, I'm moving, shaking, barely breathing, toward a tiny girl in a NICU crib who has already stolen every piece of my soul.

The NICU hums with soft beeps and quiet voices, a room built of vigilance and hope.

When the nurse leads me to her crib, my breath catches hard enough to hurt.

She is small, newborn small. Not fragile in the way of micro-preemies, but delicate in the way that anything this new feels like it could slip through your fingers if you breathe too loudly.

She is bundled in a pink blanket, tiny hat askew, one fist tucked stubbornly under her cheek. Her chest rises and falls fast but steady, the kind of breathing the nurse is saying is normal for newborns.

Grace.

My daughter.

My knees almost buckle.

I sink into the chair beside her crib, elbows on my thighs, hands trembling so badly I have to clasp them together.

"Hi," I whisper, the word breaking apart on the way out. "I'm your dad."

God. The way that shatters me.

"I thought I would meet you with your mom in my arms, yelling at me to stop fussing." My voice cracks. "I didn't think it would be like this. I didn't think you would come so fast, or that she would..."

I swallow hard. "She's still back there. They're working on her."

I press my palm gently to the side of the crib, not touching her yet, just anchoring myself to the only thing in the room that feels real.

"You're doing so well," I whisper. "They think you need a little extra watching after what happened."

Her fingers twitch.

My breath stutters.

"I missed the first few months of you," I murmur. "And that will haunt me for the rest of my life. But I swear to you, sweetheart, I'm not missing anything else. Not one second."

The words tremble out of me.

"And no matter what happens behind those doors, no matter what they come out and say about your mom..."

My throat closes. It takes everything in me to force the next words out.

"You are not losing me. You hear me? I will carry you both if I have to."

A tear falls onto my hand. Then another.

"I've got you," I whisper. "Daddy is right here. I'm not going anywhere."

I bow my head beside her crib, ruined and praying and bargaining with every god I ignored my entire life.

"Please," I choke out. "Please keep my girls safe. Both of them. Please."

And in the dim, protective glow of the NICU monitors, with Candy somewhere beyond my reach, fighting her own unseen battle, I fall apart completely, terrified and helpless, loving both of them so fiercely it feels like my heart may never fit back together the same way again.

The NICU doors swish open behind me.

Footsteps.

A pause.

"Mr. Monroe?" the doctor says.

And the world stops.

1 Year Later

Chapter Forty-One

Epilogue

Asher

Grace wakes me before the sun does.

Not crying. She seldom cries in the morning. Instead, she babbles loudly and with purpose, like she's giving a keynote speech to her stuffed animals about the geopolitical implications of turning one year old.

"MmmMmMma. Ba. Gaaaa. DADA!"

I smile into my pillow.

That last part, she knows how to use.

Weaponized adorableness.

Effective every time.

I roll out of bed and head into her room. Her room, not a NICU crib or the corner of my apartment she started in, but a real nursery in a real house. She is standing in the crib, gripping the railing with fat hands, cheeks pink and chubby, hair like spun gold sticking up in every direction.

And of course, her bluebird is clutched to her chest like it is part of her ribcage.

"Good morning, birthday girl," I murmur.

She beams. It is blinding.

"Da-da-da-DA!"

"Well, if you insist," I chuckle, scooping her up.

She smells like baby shampoo and sleep and joy. Pure joy. A year later, and it still knocks the breath out of me how small she was, how fast everything changed, how helpless I felt in those hours where nothing was guaranteed.

I kiss her forehead. She pats my cheek, then grabs my chin with surprising force.

"Gentle," I remind her.

She yanks a little harder.

"Right. Of course. Your day, your rules."

I carry her to the changing table. She drops the bluebird exactly once, which in her world is a category-five emergency.

"Oh no," I gasp. "Is Bluey okay?"

She leans so far over to retrieve him I have to anchor her with one arm.

"Ahhhh!" she scolds me.

"I apologize. I'll treat him with the respect he deserves."

Changing her is a four-round wrestling match. By the time I get her into clean pajamas, she's pulled one of her pigtails out.

"I worked hard on that," I tell her.

She grins, utterly unrepentant.

"Okay, fine. Happy birthday. You win everything today."

I carry her downstairs to the kitchen of the house I bought exactly one day after she was born. The day after the longest night of my life. The day after I fell apart beside her incubator. The day after I couldn't fix a damn thing.

So I did the only thing I could think to do. I bought a home in Candy's hometown. A quiet, traditional Goshen colonial with white shutters, a wraparound porch, maple floors, and a kitchen big enough for a future I couldn't let myself picture yet. Cash offer. Thirty-day closing.

Grace kicks her heels against my ribs as I settle her into the highchair.

"Hungry?" I ask, even though she's already reaching toward the counter where the bananas live.

"Na-na!" she shouts.

"Yes, that is the correct answer."

I mash bananas, scramble eggs, cut blueberries in half like the paranoid father I am, and place the plate in front of her.

She sweeps an entire handful directly onto the floor.

"An artistic choice," I decide.

She squeals and launches a blueberry at my shirt.

"Ah, yes. A bold statement piece."

I sip my coffee while Grace babbles through a story that absolutely has all of her attention.

"You know," I say lightly, "Meemaw and Peepaw are coming today."

She gasps dramatically, eyes huge.

"And Aunt SeeSee."

She claps.

"And you have a new dress for your party."

She grabs her bluebird and smushes him to her face in excitement, legs kicking hard enough to shake the highchair.

I lean my head on my hand and just look at her.

One year. One year of watching her learn to smile, to hold her head up, to sit, to crawl, and now to walk if she has something sturdy to cling to. One year of mornings like this. One year of gratitude I don't have words for.

She bangs her hands on the tray, babbling urgently.

"Tell me more," I say.

She babbles louder.

"And what happens next?"

She shrieks and drops a piece of egg in her lap.

"Ah. A twist ending."

I laugh and finish my coffee.

That is when I hear the front door open.

Grace freezes. Then squeals. The happy kind.

"Ma-ma-ma!"

I turn toward the entryway just as footsteps cross the threshold and Candy walks in.

The front door swings open, and before I can even stand, Grace launches into a full-body wiggle in her highchair.

"Ma-ma-ma-ma!"

Candy steps inside, arms full. A bakery box balances on one hip and a giant gift bag on the other. Her hair is twisted up haphazardly with a clip, a few curls sticking to her temple from the heat outside. The morning sun behind her makes the whole entryway glow.

She looks like summertime and home and everything warm; everything I didn't know I needed before her.

"Good morning, birthday girl!" she sings as she bumps the door closed with her hip.

Grace shrieks like Beyoncé herself just walked in.

Candy laughs, that soft, sweet sound she didn't make for months after Grace was born. The sound that still feels like winning something impossible.

She drops the bakery box onto the counter and hurries over. She kisses Grace's forehead and brushes a hand over her messy curls.

"I see Daddy let you do your own hair again," she teases.

"I tried," I say.

"You sure did," she answers with a grin that hits straight in the chest.

Grace proudly holds up her bluebird for inspection.

"Oh my goodness," Candy gasps. "Is Bluey ready for your big party?"

Grace nods so dramatically she nearly tips sideways.

Candy steadies her, presses another kiss to her cheek, then turns to me. Softer now, like something in her shifts the moment our eyes meet.

"Hey," she murmurs.

"Hey," I say.

She rises onto her toes to kiss me. A quick, warm brush of lips that tastes like sweet tea and summer air.

"You sleep okay?" she asks.

"Eventually. Your daughter began her birthday with a lecture."

"Ah." Candy nods. "Well, I'm sure you needed it."

She opens the bakery box. Inside are mini cinnamon rolls, each one glazed and glittering under the morning light.

"Party treats," she announces. "Mom and I finished everything. Dad already started the smoker."

"So business as usual," I say.

"Exactly."

Grace bangs her hands on the tray again.

"And Aunt SeeSee is on her way," Candy adds.

Grace squeals.

I lean my chin on my hand and just look at them. These two miracles. Alive. Here. Mine.

Candy wipes a smear of banana from Grace's cheek, humming softly as sunlight warms her shoulders.

She glances at the clock. "Okay, I need to shower and change before my parents show up with half of Goshen."

"And I should get Grace dressed," I say.

Candy turns slowly, and if looks could kill, I wouldn't be standing at all.

"Right before the party," I correct immediately.

She relaxes. "There he is."

She kisses Grace again, squeezes my arm, and disappears down the hall, humming softly.

I let out a long exhale I have been holding. A year ago, I didn't know if I would ever see her walk into a room again. I didn't know if mornings like this would ever exist.

Now they do.

And somewhere between banana-covered fingers and birthday cinnamon rolls, I know with perfect clarity. Today might be the day I ask her something life-changing. But first, we survive the party.

Grace slams both palms into her tray like she is urging me to get on with it.

"All right, all right," I laugh. "We'll clean you up, and then we'll go cause chaos when your grandparents get here."

She squeals.

I wipe her face, lift her from the highchair, grab Bluey, and head upstairs.

Candy emerges again, hair curled loosely, soft blue sundress floating around her knees.

She looks like the answer to every prayer I never said aloud.

"Ready?" she asks.

"Born ready."

"You were not born ready," she says. "You needed four months of baby immersion to become a competent dad."

Grace pats my cheek proudly.

"Da-da-da!"

"See? She believes in me."

Candy grins as she lifts the last tray from the counter.

"Come on," she says. "Let's get everything set up before my parents get here."

I adjust Grace on my hip, grab the stack of gift bags, and follow Candy toward the backyard.

And just like that, the party begins.

By the time we look outside, our backyard has transformed into a birthday party paradise. Balloons sway from the porch beams. Streamers ripple in the warm July breeze. The smell of smoked brisket drifts across our yard, proof that Candy's dad is already working his magic on the smoker.

Children chase bubbles under the maple tree.

Three folding tables are covered with pastel tablecloths and more casseroles than any rational human should consume.

Candy's mother spots us through the sliding door and waves wildly.

"Oh boy," Candy mutters affectionately. "She's been vibrating since sunrise."

I barely shift Grace on my hip before Meemaw swoops in and plucks her right out of my arms.

"There's my birthday angel!"

Grace shrieks in pure joy, clutching Bluey in one fist and immediately reaching for Meemaw's earrings with the other.

Candy's dad claps me on the back as he passes a platter toward the food table. "Morning, son."

I still flinch a little at the word son. Not because it's unwelcome, but because of how badly I once wished I would earn it.

"Morning," I manage.

"Ash!" Serina jogs up, wearing glitter, because, of course, she is. "I brought the bubble cannon."

"Of course you did," Candy groans.

"It is her birthday," Serina insists. "There should be chaos."

Grace agrees by screaming happily.

Guests trickle in through the side gate, neighbors, family friends, Serina's boyfriend with a stack of wrapped gifts that could financially destabilize a small country.

Candy moves through the groups effortlessly, laughing, hugging, and refilling food. I stay close, half because I want to, half because Grace is using me as a mobile perch to show off Bluey to anyone within a ten-foot radius.

Every few minutes, Candy glances over at us.

Not in a checking way.

In a this-is-my-family way.

It hits me square in the sternum every single time.

Candy's mom brings out the smash cake, pastel frosting, tiny sugar bluebirds perched on top like a confectionery aviary.

"Ready, sweetheart?" Candy whispers as she sets Grace in the highchair under the maple tree.

Grace smacks her hands on the tray.

"Da! Da!"

"She knows what's coming," Serina says proudly.

Candy kneels beside the chair. I stand behind the crowd with my phone, recording every second like the unhinged parent I have become.

Everyone sings.

Grace claps half a beat behind the rhythm, thrilled with herself.

Candy leans in to help her blow out the candle.

Or tries to.

Grace grabs the candle instead.

"Nope!" Candy squeaks, catching her hand gently. "We do not touch fire, baby."

Grace responds by face-planting directly into the cake.

The crowd erupts.

Candy looks up at me, frosting smeared across her cheek, eyes bright and warm and alive.

And looking at her like this, frosting on her cheek and joy in her eyes, the truth rises up without hesitation.

Tonight.

It takes two hours to clean up, pack gifts, wipe frosting off everything, and undress Grace, who is exhausted and sticky and chanting "Da-da-da-mamaaaa" in slurred syllables.

Candy carries her upstairs, humming softly. I follow because I don't know how not to. We get her bathed and into a fresh onesie. We read her two books and sing the song Candy made up that became our bedtime routine.

Grace's eyes flutter. Her fist curls around Bluey. Candy brushes her hair off her forehead.

"She had a perfect day," she whispers.

"She did."

We stand there a long moment, watching her melt into sleep.

Candy's hand slips into mine. Warm and familiar.

The moment settles into place. Quiet. Earned. Absolute.

I turn to her.

"Hey," I say softly.

She looks up. "What?"

I tuck a curl behind her ear. "I need to ask you something. I don't think I can wait anymore." Her breath catches, her eyes widen.

"Would you come downstairs with me?" Candy nods, sliding her hand into mine. We walk toward the moment neither of us ever thought we would get. The moment that turns our long, hard path into a beginning.

The house is quiet. Evening light spills gold across the hardwood. Her dress sways around her calves when she turns to face me.

"Asher?" she whispers.

I take a breath.

I reach into my pocket and pull out the ring box.

Candy's lips part. Her eyes shimmer.

"Before you say anything," I say, "I want you to know this is not because of today or this year or the fact that we're raising our daughter together."

I open the box. A pink diamond sparkles in the light, and Candy catches breath.

"It's because every time life knocked you down, you stood back up. It's because you let me love Grace with you, because you let me see you heal and grow into an amazing woman and mother. Because you chose me, even when you didn't have to."

Tears spill down her cheeks, and I gently wipe them away.

"I fell in love with you the first time you rolled your eyes at me and called me impossible. No one ever challenged me like that. No one ever made me want to be better," I say.

She lets out a watery laugh.

"And I never stopped. Not for one second. Not even when we were a mess. Not even when I was sure I lost you."

I take her hand.

"Candy Hart, will you marry me?"

Her answer is a gasp, a sob, a laugh.

"Yes," she whispers. Then louder, "Yes, Asher. Of course I will."

I slide the ring onto her finger. She throws her arms around my neck.

I hold her. Because a year ago, I didn't know if I would ever get to touch her again.

She kisses me.

"You locked the front door, right?" she breathes against my mouth.

"I did."

"Good."

She kisses me again, deeper this time. Her fingers curl in my shirt as I lift her. Her legs wind around me.

"Asher..."

"Mm?"

"Take me upstairs, please."

"Anything for you, my lady."

She laughs against my jaw, warm and breathless.

I lay her gently on the bed and brush a pink curl from her cheek.

"Come here," she murmurs.

So I do.

I settle over her, my weight on my elbows as I lower my head to hers. The kiss is slow and deep, a deliberate exploration. Her hands slide up my arms, over my shoulders, her fingers tangling in the hair at the nape of my neck. I groan into her mouth as her nails scrape lightly against my scalp. I break the kiss to trail my lips along her jaw, down the sensitive column of her throat. She tastes like vanilla and something uniquely Candy.

My hands find the hem of her skirt and I pause, my fingers just brushing the warm skin of her waist gently back and forth. I look down at her, her eyes dark and heavy lidded in the soft light of the room, and can't help but think about how beautiful she is. She gives a slight, almost imperceptible nod, her lips parted in anticipation. I lift the dress over her head, tossing it aside and revealing her smooth and pale skin, her breasts spilling over the top of a simple, lacy black bra. I trace the edge of the lace with my fingertip, watching as her nipples pebble beneath the thin fabric, begging for attention.

I lower my head and take one into my mouth through the lace, sucking gently, making Candy arch her back; a soft cry escaping her lips. Her hands fist in the sheets as I lavish attention on first one, then the other. The fabric is rough against my tongue, a frustrating barrier. I reach behind her, my fingers fumbling for the clasp. It comes free with a flick of my wrist, and I toss the bra to join her shirt on the floor.

Her breasts are perfect, full, and round with dusky pink nipples. I take one peak into my mouth, swirling my tongue around it before biting down gently. She gasps, her hips bucking against me. I can feel the heat radiating from her core. I move to the other breast, giving it the same treatment as my hand slides down her stomach, my fingers tracing the waistband of her panties.

I can feel the tremor that runs through her body. I lift my head to look at her again. Her cheeks are flushed, her chest rising and falling with each ragged breath.

"Asher," she whispers, her voice husky with need. "Please."

I don't make her wait any longer. I hook my fingers in the waistband of her panties, pulling them down in one smooth motion. I toss them over my shoulder, not caring where they land. She's completely bare before me, laid out like a feast. I spread her legs with my hands, my gaze fixed on the glistening pink folds of her sex.

I lower myself between her thighs, my breath warm against her. I can smell her arousal, a sweet, intoxicating scent. I run my tongue through her slick folds, and she cries out, her hips lifting off the bed. I wrap my arms around her thighs, holding her open for me as I devour her. I find her clit, a hard, sensitive nub, and flick my tongue against it again and again. I suck it into my mouth, my tongue swirling around it as I slide two fingers into her tight, wet heat.

She's so fucking tight. I curl my fingers, searching for that spot inside her that will make her scream. I find it, and she shatters. Her body convulses, her inner walls clamping down on my fingers as a wave of pleasure washes over her. I don't stop, my tongue and fingers work in tandem to draw out her orgasm, to push her higher and higher until she's a writhing, sobbing mess beneath me.

When she finally comes down, she's limp and boneless. I kiss my way back up her body, my lips leaving a trail of fire on her skin. I pause at her mouth, my own aching with need. I'm still fully dressed, my cock straining against the zipper of my jeans, a painful reminder of my own arousal.

Candy seems to sense my urgency. Her hands are suddenly everywhere, tugging at my shirt, fumbling with the button on my jeans. I help her, stripping off my clothes in a frenzy of need. My cock springs free, hard and thick, the tip already leaking with pre-cum.

I settle back over her, my body covering hers. I can feel the heat of her against my sensitive skin. I look into her eyes, and what I see there takes my breath away. It's not just lust, but something deeper, something more profound. It's trust. It's vulnerability. It's love.

I position myself at her entrance, the head of my cock nudging against her wet folds. "Are you ready for me, Candy?" I ask, my voice rough with emotion.

She wraps her legs around my waist, pulling me closer. "I've been ready for you my whole life," she whispers.

That's all the encouragement I need. I push into her, slow and steady, giving her time to adjust to my size. She's so tight, so wet, so fucking perfect. I groan as I sink deeper and deeper, until I'm buried to the hilt inside her. I stay still for a moment, savoring the feeling of being joined with her, of being one with her.

Then I start to move. My strokes are long and slow at first, a gentle rocking motion that builds the tension between us. I can feel her muscles tightening around me, hear her soft moans of pleasure in my ear. I pick up the pace, my thrusts becoming harder, faster, more demanding. I'm no longer in control, driven by a primal need to claim her, to possess her, to make her mine.

The room is filled with the slap of skin against skin, our ragged breaths, my whispered words of encouragement and endearment. I can feel my own release building, a tight coil in my gut. I reach between us, my fingers finding her clit. I rub it in tight circles, matching the rhythm of my thrusts.

"Asher," she cries out, her body tensing. "Oh god, Asher!"

Her orgasm rips through her, and she shatters around me, her inner walls clamping down on my cock like a vise. The sensation is too much. With a guttural roar, I follow her over the edge, my own release tearing through me. I pour myself into her, my body shaking with the force of my climax.

I collapse on top of her, body spent, heart hammering against my ribs. I bury my face in the crook of her neck, breathing in her scent. We lie there for a long time, our bodies tangled together, our breathing slowly returning to normal.

I roll off her, pulling her into my arms. She snuggles against my chest, her head on my shoulder. I stroke her hair, my fingers tracing the path of her spine.

"I love you, Candy," I whisper into the quiet of the room.

She lifts her head, her eyes shining with unshed tears. "I love you too, Asher."

And in that moment, I know. This is it. This is everything.

Afterward, she lies against my chest, tracing circles over my sternum, her ring glinting in the lamplight.

"Hey," she whispers.

"Yeah?"

"Do you know what I thought about this morning when I was picking up the pastries?"

"What is that?"

"How lucky Grace is to have a dad who loves her like this."

My throat tightens, but I refuse to cry.

"And you," she adds. "Do you know how lucky you are?"

I raise a brow. "Oh? Enlighten me."

She grins. "You get to marry me."

I laugh. "I accept my fate."

She settles against me again, breath warm against my skin.

As the house grows quiet, as the air cools and the sun fades, it hits me.

Every fear. Every sleepless night. Every cliff we almost fell off. It all led here.

She's in my arms.

Our daughter is asleep upstairs.

A ring is on her finger.

A future we built from the wreckage waits for us.

She kisses my chest softly.

"I love you," she whispers.

I close my eyes, hold her tighter, and answer with the truest words I have ever spoken.

"I love you too. Both of my girls. Always."

And for the first time in my entire life, forever feels easy.

Chapter Forty-Two

Also by

The Wild Child Reckless Series

This is Growing Up

She was his best friend's little sister and completely off-limits—until one unforgettable night changed everything. Now Delilah is famous, engaged, and untouchable... but Alexander isn't giving up that easily. Because he had her once, and he's not letting her go again.

This is Meant to Be

She's promised to another. He's risking everything to keep her. Lillian was never supposed to fall for Jensen—but now that she has, neither of them is willing to let go, no matter how high the price.

This is Taking Chances

He shattered her heart once. Now he's back—not just to make amends, but to prove he's worthy of the family he never knew he had. A deaf drummer with a broken past. A single mother who swore she'd never look back. One love story that refuses to stay buried.

This is Starting Over**

She was the one girl he swore off limits. Now she's all grown up, in danger—and back under his protection.

This time, he's not sure he can walk away.

Foster, Inc. Novellas

Jack Frost, CEO

She's his assistant. He's her father's enemy. Pretending to be engaged might save his business deal, but when sparks turn into something real, Jack has to decide if falling for Maisie is worth the risk—or the scandal.

Willow Glen Series

From Feud to Forever*

She stole the land he spent twenty years trying to reclaim. He's determined to make her regret it—until their bickering turns into banter and the sparks start flying. In a small town full of gossip and grudge matches, Adam and Christiane are about to find out that the line between hate and love is thinner than a fence post.

A Highland Homestead Christmas**

Also part of the Piper Falls Christmas Collection

She came to Texas to settle her stepfather's estate. He only meant to stop by for a cow. By one fake engagement, a meddling town, and a feud-hungry uncle later, Mharie Campbell and Patrick Williams are knee-deep in Christmas chaos–and each other. In Piper Falls, where traditions fun deep and every secret sparks a rumor, they'll have to decide if what started as pretend is worth keeping for real.

Anything But Ordinary**

He likes life simple and quiet. She was the girl who once blew it wide open. Now Laney Brooks is back in Willow Glen—older, braver, and dragging a chaos-loving yellow lab straight into Brandon Williams's carefully ordered world. In a town where memories run deep and second chances don't come easy, these former sweethearts will have to decide if the love they lost is worth fighting for... or finally letting go.

Sons of Santoro Series

Tasting Sin-

Also part of the Sexy as Sin: Las Vegas World

She's the boss with everything to lose. He's the chef with nothing left to prove.

When a high-stakes sabotage threatens Sienna Moreau's Las Vegas hotel, she turns to the one man who infuriates and tempts her in equal measure—Luca Santoro. In a city built on secrets, desire becomes their sharpest weapon... but trusting each other might be the biggest gamble of all.

Monroe Strategic Capital Series

The Christmas Waffle*

He's a grumpy CEO with a plan for everything. She's the too-young, off-limits assistant who blows it all to hell with one unforgettable night—and one life-changing surprise. Now, with secrets, misunderstandings, and a baby on the line, they'll have to decide if their second chance is worth risking everything for.

*2025 $0.99 Preorder

** 2026 $0.99 Preorder

Chapter Forty-Three

From the Author

Thank you for reading!!! If you have a moment please leave a review- they are so incredibly important to indie authors. I always loved reading, and now I have a separate love of writing. I hope you stick around and join me in this amazing adventure! I am always looking to connect! You can find me in the following places.

SmutTok Made Me Do It Facebook Group

Juliet McKinleys Book Nook

Sign Up for my newsletter here so that you never miss a beat, giveaway or sneak peek-

Newsletter   julietmckinley.myflodesk.com

TikTok   @JulieyMcKinleyAuthor

Instagram   @JulietMckinleyAuthor

Facebook   Juliet McKinley